CONSTABLE AT THE DAM

The construction of a dam and reservoir brings a new set of problems to the resident constable of Aidensfield. Claude Jeremiah Greengrass creates concern when he finds a skeleton, and Florrie the shoplifter gives police and shopkeepers a run for their money. Meanwhile, Nick ponders the will of the eccentric Warwick Humbert Ravenswood, whose last wish is to be buried at the bottom of the new reservoir. However, the artist, Gordon Precious gives Nick his greatest challenge when he vows to destroy the dam and reservoir—and steals a cache of explosives to carry out his threat!

CONSTABLE AT THE DAM

by
Nicholas Rhea

Magna Large Print Books
Long Preston, North Yorkshire,
England.

British Library Cataloguing in Publication Data.

Rhea, Nicholas
    Constable at the dam.

A catalogue record for this book is
available from the British Library

ISBN 0-7505-1309-8

First published in Great Britain by Robert Hale Ltd., 1997

Published in Large Print 1998 by arrangement with Robert
Hale Ltd.

Magna Large Print is an imprint of
Library Magna Books Ltd.
Printed and bound in Great Britain by
T.J. International Ltd., Cornwall, PL28 8RW.

1

We must grant the artist his subject, his
  idea, his *donné:*
our criticism is applied only to what he
  makes of it.
                                    Henry James (1843–1916)

Gordon Precious was a very quiet and
unobtrusive man, the sort you'd never
notice in a crowd or at a party and it
was some time before I knew his name or
realized he was a resident of Aidensfield.
I think I became aware of him around the
time I heard news that a dam and reservoir
were to be constructed in Ramsdale. That
is a beautiful but remote valley some
two miles north-west of Aidensfield and
the links between Gordon Precious and
Ramsdale became increasingly dramatic
during my passage of time as the village
constable. Indeed, those links continued
virtually throughout the whole of my service
in Aidensfield.

So far as Gordon was concerned, he was
not the sort to come to the notice of the
police in any form, good or bad, and I

did not encounter him during my leisure moments either. One of those anonymous people who travelled to work daily from Aidensfield to Ashfordly, he queued for Arnold Merryweather's bus every morning and returned at teatime to spend his leisure periods indoors or perhaps in his modest garden. Although I'd noticed him at the bus stop, it was a long time before I knew Gordon's name because he took no part in village activities. He never volunteered to work on committees or help with social events; he never popped into the pub for a drink neither did he join the cricket team or play billiards in the village hall.

I'd never seen him drive a car or ride a bike, nor did he attend any of the churches or even walk a dog. Even so, not once did I regard him as snobbish or aloof—I concluded he was a very shy, reserved and modest gentleman.

In his early forties, of average build with wavy brown hair and glasses, Gordon would wait for the bus in his dull brown suit and would never talk to anyone. That's how I first noticed him, a solitary brown figure who could be observed in all weathers waiting to catch Arnold's morning omnibus—provided Arnold had managed to get his creaking old bus to start.

Because I noticed Gordon so regularly

at the bus stop, my interest gradually increased. I did not know what he did for a living or how he occupied his spare time and I never saw him at any other place in the village. I never even noticed him walking to or from the bus stop! Because I saw him there and nowhere else, he became something of an enigma and I wondered where he spent the rest of his time or how he earned his living. I thought there must be more to life than waiting for Arnold Merryweather's bus.

Such inbred curiosity is part of the work of a village constable; it is a means of getting to know members of the community, a method which fills a mental filing system which may or may not have some future use. As my interest deepened, I accepted I had no professional reason to probe the life of the quiet brown man and must admit it was with some surprise I discovered he had a wife. It had taken some time to establish a link between the inconspicuous bus-catcher and the rather glamorous blonde woman I'd often noticed around Aidensfield.

I'd also seen her serving behind the bar of the Hopbind Inn at Elsinby. This is precisely the kind of gradually acquired local knowledge that a village constable assimilates during the course of his work; it is not regarded as spying upon individuals but simply the result of the observations of events which are part of one's daily routine. Any villager would acquire similar knowledge.

My first positive link between the blonde barmaid and the brown bus-stop man came with an item of found property. Mrs Precious—Deirdre to her friends—found a small blue leather purse lying in the street at Aidensfield and, after fruitlessly enquiring in the post office after a possible loser, she brought it to me. It contained £5 in mixed notes and coins, but there was nothing to indicate the name of the loser. Deirdre opted not to retain the purse at her home because she worked and was away from the house a lot of the time; her husband was out all day too. If the loser was a pensioner who urgently wanted its return, then it would be better left at my police house. I agreed and entered the find in my Found Property register. I told Deirdre it would become her property if it was not claimed within three months, but as things worked out, an elderly lady in the village did report the loss that very same day. I was delighted that the purse and its contents were so rapidly restored to the grateful loser and I supplied her with Deirdre's name and address. It was my small-talk with the friendly Deirdre during that small incident which

8

established that Mrs Deirdre Precious was the wife of Gordon, the man at the bus stop. I discovered they lived at Glebe Cottage, Aidensfield and that he worked as a clerk for Ashfordly Rural District Council, dealing with the issue of licenses of various kinds.

I learned that Gordon caught Arnold Merryweather's bus to work every morning just before half past eight. That's when all the miscellaneous snippets of information gleaned during my duties came together. As I mentally noted the man at the bus stop was called Gordon Precious. Deirdre told me he had a good steady job with security for life, even if it did lack any glamour, excitement or prospects for promotion. She added she had a part-time post in a ladies' fashion shop in Ashfordly in addition to her bar work and she used the family car to drive herself to her various jobs. And so, in that rather oblique way, I discovered the identity of the quiet man in the brown suit who so diligently patronized Arnold Merryweather's bus service.

Deirdre was a most attractive woman and I guessed she would be in her late thirties. She had a mass of blonde hair, fine legs and a very well-endowed figure which she usually managed to display to advantage. She was blessed with an outgoing personality which complemented her buxom appearance. Some might say she dressed rather flashily, or in the manner of a woman five or ten years younger than she really was, or that she used too much make-up and nail varnish, or that she wore skirts which were too short even by sixties' standards while revealing a pair of fine thighs—but few could deny she was very glamorous and personable.

The next link in the story came through an art exhibition at Ashfordly Town Hall. Organized by the local arts club, it featured the work of artists who were living or painting in the Ashfordly area.

The exhibits were chiefly watercolours and oils, albeit with a few select sculptures, and the exhibition had been staged to run from noon one Friday in March until 5 p.m. the following Sunday. As I was off duty that Friday evening, with our four children being cared for by one of their grandmothers, Mary and I went along to the preview. Upon entering, I was quite surprised to see Deirdre Precious, dressed to kill, standing before some of the paintings on display. She was accompanied by the quiet man in the brown suit whom I'd noticed at the bus stop, the man I now knew to be her husband. That evening, however, he had discarded his suit and was almost unrecognizable in his casual sweater and jeans. I went across to thank

Deirdre for handing in the purse she'd found and explained how the delighted loser had been reunited with her property. Deirdre said the old lady had dropped a postcard through her letter-box by way of thanks. It was after that initial chat that she introduced me to Gordon, her shy husband. That was our first meeting.

'Gordon, this is PC Rhea, and Mrs Rhea.'

'Call me Nick,' I invited, smiling at the reticent man as I held out my hand for him to shake. 'I've seen you at Aidensfield bus stop.'

'Yes, I work in Ashfordly, at the council offices.' He spoke very quietly, taking my hand in a firm grip.

'I'm Mary,' smiled my wife, emulating me by shaking Gordon's hand and then his wife's.

'You've come to buy something, or just to look?' I opened the conversation with that not-too-inspiring sentence.

'Oh, neither,' oozed Deirdre, full of pride. 'No, Gordon is an exhibitor, these are his work, those watercolours behind us. He's exhibiting twelve moorland scenes which depict the seasons or the moods of the moor.'

'Oh, I see! I had no idea you were an artist, Gordon.'

In this way, I gave him an opportunity to

11

speak for himself. 'Well, I'm not really,' he blushed. 'I'm just a clerk, but I do like to paint, it is my hobby, you see, but Deirdre thought I should try to sell some of my work.'

'He wouldn't have bothered if I hadn't persuaded him ...' she said with considerable force.

'I'm not one for pushing myself forward,' he tried.

Deirdre interrupted. 'Our house is full of his watercolours, hundreds of them, so I thought it was time he made himself known. He spends all his spare time painting. I told him to join this exhibition; his work's as good as any of the others, if not better. He has ambitions, you know, to be a full-time artist ... he just needs a push in the right direction. I know he's good enough. The trouble is he won't take the plunge or even try to sell his work. Sometimes, I wish he'd have the nerve to give up that dead-end job with the council and try to earn his living by painting. He's wasted there; he's talented. He's good enough to be a professional, don't you think?'

'If that is what he wants, then I am sure he will succeed,' I said cautiously. 'And yes, I do think his work is very good.'

Although I am no expert in any kind of art, I was not lying.

12

I did like Gordon's work but I knew it was very difficult to earn a living as a full-time artist, irrespective of one's talent. But it was not impossible. Talent combined with a businesslike approach meant a good living could be made from the arts. If Gordon did launch himself as an artist, Deirdre might have to find more lucrative work to support him, but I reckoned she was the sort of woman who would do that. During that modest exhibition, I found myself admiring Gordon's highly atmospheric paintings. Some were very sombre or even dark and gloomy but he had a wonderful way of capturing the silent threat and utter stillness of the remote moorlands. He was able to capture their ability to terrify or surprise those who ventured upon their brooding and bleak wastes. Some of the skies he portrayed were overtly hostile with their deep grey clouds and lack of sunshine; in some ways, his work could be quite frightening and I wondered if it revealed anything of his deeper personality, moods or frustrations.

After studying several watercolours, I reserved a fine painting of Ramsdale as viewed from High Cross Rigg. It depicted Ramsdale's famous stone cross as it stood among purple heather in the foreground. In the distant background was

13

the shallow-bottomed dale beneath one of Gordon's dark and brooding skies, while the slender silver ribbon of Ramsdale Beck twisted along the floor of the dale. Alders and willows lined its route and a sunbeam highlighted the pale limestone of the ancient pack-horse bridge which spanned the beck. That beautiful bridge, known as Ramsdale Bridge, carried the centuries-old track which wound its way around the dale head. Prominent in the centre of the picture was a solitary deserted house.

It stood empty beside the track as it meandered into the upper reaches of the dale. A sturdy former farmhouse, it had an air of neglect combined with character and strength. In that remote moorland dale beneath a dark sky, the house appeared as a haven of refuge from any oncoming storm. That was something Gordon managed to capture to perfection.

I liked the painting for the atmosphere it created and it continues to hang in our lounge. It is also the reminder of a memorable sequence of events which developed and concluded during my tenure at Aidensfield.

It would be about a year after that art exhibition that all rural constables in Ashfordly Section were summoned to a meeting in the police station at 10 a.m.

14

one April morning. It was a Wednesday and we were to be addressed by Sergeant Blaketon on what he would only describe as a matter of some importance. At the appointed time, I went along and joined my colleagues. Alf Ventress had managed to produce ten cups of a peculiar light greyish liquid which he claimed was coffee. Most of it was sloshing around in cracked mugs which the prisoners used if and when we placed any of them in the cells, but on the credit side Alf's concoction was warm, wet and welcome.

We squeezed into Sergeant Blaketon's cramped office; there was nowhere to sit so we stood in an untidy group while he counted heads and ticked names off his list. Satisfied that we were all present, he settled in his chair, placed his elbows on the desk, linked his hands as if in prayer and looked sternly at us.

Clearly, he was about to impart words of great wisdom.

'I have called this meeting for a very good reason,' he began. 'We, that is all the police officers of Ashfordly Section, are to be tested in a way that befalls few sections as small as ours. The population of Aidensfield is to be greatly increased by people whom I fear may not prove very savoury. These incomers will be living, working and enjoying their leisure time

15

among us for several years to come.'

'Aidensfield, Sergeant?' I was not sure I had heard him correctly. To my knowledge, there was no planned housing development in the village.

'Yes, PC Rhea. Aidensfield. Your village, your patch. The rural beat for which you are responsible.'

'So what's going to happen?' I interrupted him.

'I am coming to that, Rhea, if you will permit me. The cause of this change is a new reservoir. Those of you who bother to read the papers will have seen references to this project—it has been under discussion for several years and has been subjected to all manner of objections from naturalists, farmers, landowners and others. But, stage by stage, every objection has been dealt with and the outcome is that the reservoir is going to be built, along with a new dam. Work will begin immediately and the official announcement will appear in tomorrow's Press. That means we can expect a lot of fuss, perhaps with demonstrations by conservationists and even rent-a-mob, and an inevitable increase in our workload. But it is too late for further objections at this stage. Any demonstrations will be a waste of time, Ramsdale Bridge Reservoir will be built. There is no doubt about that.'

16

He paused for effect, then continued, 'It has been commissioned by Swanland Corporation to supply their future needs both for domestic use and for industry. It will be constructed in Ramsdale, or to be precise, in upper Ramsdale. As I said just now, that lies on Aidensfield beat. There is a natural depression in the upper reaches of Ramsdale, the underlying strata of which is ideal to support a lake of considerable size and volume. A large dam will be built across the narrow section of the dale to contain the flow from the moors. That's what's going to happen. The work will take several years—five years has been quoted as a likely timescale but it might take longer if the workmen indulge in their current hobby of striking because they don't get a tea break or if the water's cold in their toilet washbasins. On the other hand, the construction period might be of shorter duration if no undue problems arise and if the workforce actually do what they are paid to do when they are supposed to do it. Men, equipment, earth-moving machines, diggers, lorries, cranes and almost anything and anyone who's needed to dig large holes and shift mountains of earth, along with temporary site offices, toilets and perhaps some living accommodation for the workmen, will be moving into the area immediately.'

Although I had long known of the proposed reservoir, I had no idea it was so close to being built; furthermore, I had no idea how it would affect my hitherto peaceful rural life. But Sergeant Blaketon was continuing and he provided some idea of the problems I might have to face.

'There is no doubt construction workers will descend in large numbers upon our pubs and upon unattached young women during their free time. They'll have money to spend and will not be afraid to spend it locally, even if much of it is recycled through the pubs to be eventually flushed down the drain. Some cash might find its way into the shops and betting offices, so there could be benefits to the local economy. Because these men will have more spending money than our local lads, I fear the locals will not take kindly to well-paid incomers attracting the more impressionable of the available women. Fights will surely follow; maidens will fall to the temptation of lust disguised as love. It is a sad world for such young ladies, but life can be cruel at times. Our duties will have to take into account additional work from a variety of sources and I fear we are heading for a busy, but rather interesting, time.'

I thought his forecast was too pessimistic although we could expect some problems.

That was inevitable. Like all local residents, I had long been aware of the protracted plans to turn upper Ramsdale into a reservoir. Over the years, there had been a rash of articles and features in the local papers, with meetings in village halls and protestations to Parliament and the local councils. And there had been a modest success. As Sergeant Blaketon spoke, I could dimly recall some of the local antagonism—indeed one man, whose name had meant nothing to me at the time, had won an important battle to save some rare flowers which flourished on a patch of land close to the proposed shoreline. His win meant the water-level would be lower than first planned.

Speculation about the proposed reservoir and dam had been rife for years, the first hint arising long before I came to Aidensfield. Because references had been few in recent months, however, the story had slipped from public consciousness, consequently the likelihood of a new reservoir had been relegated to the back of my mind.

But I couldn't escape it now. It was a reality and it was going to be virtually on my doorstep. Sergeant Blaketon's reference to Ramsdale reminded me of Gordon Precious's painting which was hanging in my lounge. It depicted the dale as I knew it, unspoilt and undeveloped, little changed over the centuries. But change was coming, and it was coming fast. Ramsdale's beautiful landscape would vanish beneath an artificial lake and the entire dale would be permanently transformed; tourists who had come to walk the moors or study the wild life, would be replaced by those who came to water ski or to sail their boats. The music of curlews and skylarks would be replaced with that of The Beatles and The Rolling Stones. Shops and offices would appear where heather and gorse had once reigned. The painting I had bought from Gordon Precious would therefore be a pleasing reminder of Ramsdale's former glory.

It was while listening to Sergeant Blaketon and subconsciously recalling the purchase of that picture, that I realized it was some time since I had seen Gordon and his brown suit at Arnold Merryweather's bus stop. As I pondered his absence, I also realized that Deirdre had not been enlivening the village with her short skirts, wide smiles and friendly chatter. She still worked behind the bar at the Hopbind Inn; I'd seen her there once or twice but in the few words we'd exchanged, she'd never mentioned any change in her family circumstances. Even so, I wondered where Gordon had gone; perhaps he'd got another job?

But my musings were interrupted by Sergeant Blaketon. In his familiar tones, he was continuing 'For those not familiar with the geography of Ramsdale, it lies a couple of miles to the north-west of Aidensfield as the crow flies. Through it flows Ramsdale Beck which is the excellent source of water for the new reservoir because it has many small tributaries over a wide watershed. To capture that water, the dam will be built across the dale at this point,' and he indicated a place on his wall map.

We strained forward to look. The site of the dam was where the minor unsurfaced lane crossed the dale via the ancient pack-horse bridge, known as Ramsdale Bridge. In recent memory, that old bridge had served ramblers and a herd of dairy cows which had crossed the beck at milking time, but it was too narrow for modern traffic. Now, the cows had gone and even ramblers were barred from the dale; it meant the bridge was rarely used and it was precisely on the site for the new dam.

Blaketon was saying, 'The proposed demolition of the old bridge caused an outcry so Ramsdale Bridge will be removed stone by stone and rebuilt elsewhere. In that way, it will be preserved. The dam will occupy the site of the bridge and it

21

will span the entire valley. The area above that old bridge as we view it now will be flooded. It will produce a reservoir one and a half miles long by three-quarters of a mile wide at the widest point, here,' and he stabbed the map again. 'The dam itself will be thirty feet high, and the water at its deepest point will be twenty-five feet deep when the reservoir is full. That's a lot of water. And when the reservoir is complete, it will become a tourist attraction which will bring in more people and more traffic. And therefore more work for us.'

'There's no village in the dale, is there?' pointed out Alf Ventress.

'No. There's only a narrow unsurfaced lane which circles the dale and runs across the pack-horse bridge—it's little more than a footpath in the higher reaches. There's a deserted farmhouse too, with some outbuildings. That's beside the lane where it is wider—it's called Ramsdale House. There are sundry other ruined barns, dry-stone walls and other relics of man, however. The dale used to be rich farmland but it has been untouched since Swanland purchased it years ago. Eventually, the green lane around the dale will be widened and surfaced to provide a route around the shores of the new lake. The old farmhouse will survive and the level of water, when the dam is complete, will rise to within a few feet of that road and house. Thus a picturesque lake will be created and it is envisaged it will become a centre for those wishing to indulge in water sports, nature study and other leisure activities.'

'That house is the only one in the upper dale,' I commented.

'Yes, it's the only dwelling in the upper dale. No houses, farms, churches, chapels or graveyards will be submerged, which is why Swanland Corporation were able to get approval for their plan. As work begins, therefore, there will be a lot of activity in the dale including the part which will be flooded but the chief centre of activity will be around the new dam. That's where a temporary settlement of site offices and workmen's huts will be assembled.'

'Do we know how many workers will come?' I asked.

'I have tried to get precise figures from both the Corporation and the contractors—Marchant French—but neither will commit themselves. They would only say it will be upwards of a hundred, fluctuating between as low as fifty and as high as two hundred, depending upon the work being undertaken at any given time. Although this will not be a particularly large reservoir, it will create work for us and it's going to be on your beat, Rhea.'

Although some of the work-force would be permanent, there'd be an interchange of personnel, some working on specialist activities with others undertaking the ongoing labouring work. Many of the workmen would be subcontractors or members of a travelling work-force who specialized in the construction or maintenance of dams and reservoirs. They would be drafted in as and when required. There'd also be an injection of local people who'd be hired for any tasks that might arise.

Many dams were being constructed at that time, both in the United Kingdom and overseas, while lots of those built earlier were being subjected to rigid inspections under the 1930 Reservoirs (Safety Provisions) Act. I wasn't quite sure how the legalities of dam construction would involve me but felt there would be official scrutineers and other officials who would supervise the progress of the construction. Most certainly, that was not part of my duties.

'I'm sure we will cope, Sergeant,' I said. 'From a daily point of view, the site is well away from Aidensfield, so the village itself will not be too greatly inconvenienced.'

'There'll be an increase in heavy traffic, probably at odd hours of the day or night,'

24

he reminded me. 'And the pubs on your beat will prove popular, I've no doubt, as well as those in Ashfordly and nearby. Let's hope we don't get fights and riots over women, that's the usual result of having an army of construction workers living and working in a compact area. Now, I have some handouts for you all, giving information about the contractors and the name of the persons in charge of various departments. Names of supervisors and responsible persons are given, along with phone numbers and addresses. If there are any major problems, deal with them through me or in my absence, through Sub-Divisional Headquarters. Among your papers there is a projected schedule, a scale map of the reservoir and other data. Take it and study it, then let's hope we can absorb the additional workload without hindering our heavy responsibilities to the people of this district.'

There were murmurs of agreement as we all received our paperwork, and afterwards Sergeant Blaketon addressed me. 'Rhea, I think you and I should take a tour around the proposed site. We need to familiarize ourselves with its geography before the work-force arrives.'

'A good idea, Sergeant,' I said.

'Right, we'll go immediately,' and he reached for his cap.

2

The Lord sitteth above the water flood;
and the Lord remaineth a King for
ever.

Psalms xxix. 9

Sergeant Blaketon was unfamiliar with
Ramsdale so he ordered me to drive the
official car. If the bodywork got scratched
by thorns in the narrow lanes or if the car
lost its exhaust through being grounded
on the rough, unsurfaced roads, then I
would be responsible. Such is the subtlety
of sergeants.

Unperturbed by this heavy responsibility,
I drove from Ashfordly Police Station and
after twenty minutes or so we approached
the distinctive outline of Ramsdale Cross.
This tall stone cross dominated the horizon
as we motored along High Cross Rigg and
I suggested we halt beside it, assuring
Sergeant Blaketon that it would provide
us with an elevated and very useful view
of the dale below. In particular, it would
reveal the upper reaches which had been
earmarked for the new reservoir and we'd

also see the unmade road which encircled the dale and which would one day provide a route around the entire circumference of the new lake. He'd value a knowledge of its route in case we had to use it during an emergency. I told him we'd be able to see Ramsdale's old pack-horse bridge too, a nostalgic sight during its final days of spanning the beck.

Standing in the shadow of the tall stone cross and looking into the dale which was spread before us, I found myself thinking of the picture painted by Gordon Precious.

I wondered if he was going to capture the final days of Ramsdale Bridge—I hoped he would. In the painting I had bought, Gordon had depicted not only the bridge but the entire dale and, by painting it from the very point of view we were now using, he had caught a grim moodiness we were not experiencing in the bright sunshine. Gazing at the scene he had painted so well, we could see the silvery glint of the Ramsdale Beck as it snaked between alders and willows, and we could view the high backcloth of the heathery, treeless moors which surrounded the dale. Crossing the humpbacked bridge was a length of the rough lane which circled the upper reaches of the dale, while the large deserted house stood beside the lane midway along the eastern escarpment. It was all in Gordon's painting, but we had music too. The sound of a soaring skylark singing beautifully somewhere in the heavens reached us, and a red grouse chattered angrily in the heather, protesting at our presence. We stood in silence for a few minutes to absorb the stunning view and the wild splendour of the dale. For some time, the grouse continued to grumble and I guessed it had a nest concealed nearby; probably, we had disturbed it on the nest or while tending its brood of chicks.

'You realize some people would pay a fortune to enjoy this view.' Sergeant Blaketon was clearly impressed by what he could see. 'You don't get views like this in the south. Tourists, hikers and the like would love it. And we're getting paid for standing here.'

'It's times like this I think a rural policeman has the finest job in the world,' I said. 'All this fresh air, beautiful scenery and wild life about us ...'

'Soon to be disrupted by mechanical shovels, earth-moving machines and drunken yobbos ...' he grinned. 'But, yes, let's enjoy it while we can.'

Before resuming our patrol, however, I realized the lonely Ramsdale House was occupied. Smoke was rising from its chimney and there was a line of washing

28

fluttering in the strong moorland breeze.

'There's someone in that house!' I pointed to the rising smoke.

'So, what's unusual about that?' asked Sergeant Blaketon.

'I thought it was deserted,' I told him. 'Certainly, it's always been empty while I've been patrolling the area.'

'Well, this dale's going to become very busy,' he said. 'It might be one of the construction workers who's found a nice quiet place. A case of first come, first served, I reckon.'

'If so, he's been quick off the mark!' I commented.

'Someone with inside knowledge perhaps? Who does it belong to, that house?' asked Blaketon.

'Swanland Corporation.' I wanted to show Blaketon I knew a good deal about this reservoir project. 'They bought most of the dale some ten or twelve years ago, when the estate sold those parts it owned. A few parcels of land remained in private hands, though, and one of them contained rare flowers. The corporation had the dale earmarked as a possible site for a reservoir years ago, although there were the inevitable objections which resulted in several alternative schemes. Some bits of land in the high dale were not estate-owned and if my memory is accurate, it was a crop of rare wild flowers which determined the final agreed water-level. All this happened long before I was posted to Aidensfield but because I was born and bred hereabouts, I was aware of the proposal even if I had no idea of its timescale. The fate of that house was aired when the objections were first being considered; there was early talk of it being submerged. It has remained empty all this time and it is very remote, as you can see, with no surfaced road leading to it. I'm not even sure whether it has electricity, running water or flush toilets. At first, the corporation refused to rent it to a tenant because no one knew, with any certainty in those early days, where the water-line would be or when, if ever, the dam would be built. They didn't want a sitting tenant who might refuse to quit when the water began to rise! If the dam had been bigger, the water-level would have been considerably higher and the house would have been submerged although I think it would have been demolished for reasons of safety of those practising water sports.'

'So the objectors won a partial battle by ensuring the water would rise only to an agreed lower level?'

'Yes, they did. Those rare flowers in the upper dale will survive above the water line. I remember the fuss before I came to Aidensfield. I can't remember the name of the chap involved, but he did battle with the authorities and won because of the rare flowers on his land. I remember thinking at the time it was a name which was very apt for his campaign but can't recall it now. People called it flower power! The house will be on the edge of the new lake and it'll command wonderful views across the water, a perfect place for a country lover or a water-sports fanatic.'

'Somebody got in there pretty quickly, even though they'll have to tolerate years of disturbance from the construction work,' said Blaketon, as he watched the rising smoke. 'A small price to pay for eventual peace, perhaps?'

'I'd like to check it out,' I said. 'Just to make sure it is someone who's got permission to be there, not campers, squatters or a bunch of hippies.'

'A good idea, and I want to see where the main site offices will be. I'll have to draft an operation order to deal with any emergency that might arise and there's also the security aspect to consider. We don't want valuable construction equipment being damaged by vandals, tools being nicked from our patch or wage snatches, do we, Rhea? That's the sort of thing that plays havoc with crime figures!'

'You'll be discussing security with the

contractors when they arrive?' I put to him.

'I will. They'll employ their own security staff but it's important we establish working links with the contractors.'

'I'll take you down now,' I said, pointing to a steep incline which led through the heather.

When we arrived in Ramsdale, the area set aside for the site offices and other amenities had already been cleared and levelled and it was identified with yellow-painted marker posts. There were no workmen present at this stage, however, and no vehicles, merely evidence of their fairly recent presence. We noted the route around the dale was passable but only just. In wet weather or in conditions of snow, it would cause problems unless it was properly surfaced. Even a vehicle as light as a small motor car would sink into the muddy surface.

'There are plans to upgrade that green lane provided the legal hurdles can be overcome,' Sergeant Blaketon said. 'The conservationists weren't too happy about it, but if this place is going to generate traffic both during and after the construction work, then this route must be surfaced and widened and made able to cope with emergency vehicles. I'll submit a report to the Highways Department.'

I felt sure such considerations had already been proposed—and I guessed Sergeant Blaketon would be aware of them—but a nudge from the local police might just expedite matters.

We tried to visualize the appearance of this beautiful dale with the huge dam in position and acres of fresh water spreading across the landscape. It was not an easy picture to conjure from the present scenario but our visit was useful from an operational point of view. We were sure that a sturdy security fence would be constructed to safeguard valuable vehicles and equipment while they were not in use, and I knew this would be the first of many visits I would make during the forthcoming months.

'Right, now for the house,' said the sergeant. 'You know that if it is squatters, you've no right to eject them? That's up to the owners to sort out, it's not a police matter, unless there's likely to be a breach of the peace during any ejection process. And your duty is only to prevent a breach of the peace; you don't take sides.'

'Yes, I know that,' I said. 'But at least I can alert the owners if people are occupying their property without authority.'

In the little black Ford Anglia, we bounced slowly along the unmade track and could see that the surface had been disturbed by the passage of at least two motor vehicles. Although grass was growing down the centre of the track, there were two sets of tyre marks, one the width of a small motor car and the other suggesting something wider, like a small lorry. As we approached the house, the lane passed behind it, and the wider tracks continued into the upper dale. The car's tyre marks came from a paddock at the side of the house; clearly, a vehicle was normally housed there.

'One vehicle's gone further up the dale,' I commented.

'Yes, but there's no vehicle at the house.' Sergeant Blaketon pointed to an open gate through which the muddy tyre tracks could be seen in a spacious yard before an outbuilding which served as a garage. The floor of the outbuilding was made from sandstone and it had no door. 'Maybe our journey's wasted?'

'The washing's still out,' I reminded him. 'So it seems someone might be here, a woman perhaps.'

'Pull up; we'll check it while we're here,' he said.

In the yard, we eased the little car to a halt and climbed out. A gate led through a high stone wall to the front of the sturdy stone-built house and, even as we strode towards the door, I could smell wood smoke. It was rising from the chimney. There was a sandstone path along the side of the house and we strode towards the front door which boasted a honeysuckle-covered rustic porch. Rambler roses straggled upon the house wall at either side to form a picturesque entrance.

We paused for a moment to enjoy the view over what would become the new lake and I could hear a curlew crying somewhere out of sight. But the occupant had either heard or seen our arrival and was waiting at the open door.

It was Gordon Precious.

No longer was he wearing a sombre brown suit but was dressed in casual jeans, a bright red T-shirt and open-toed sandals. He looked infinitely more relaxed than when I'd noticed him waiting daily at the bus stop.

'Oh, hello, Gordon,' I smiled a greeting. 'What a surprise!'

'Oh, hello, Mr Rhea.' He did not use my Christian name, perhaps because Sergeant Blaketon was present or perhaps because he did not know me too well. 'What brings the Force here? Am I in trouble?'

'No, not at all,' I said. 'We've been making an inspection of the site of the new dam, we have to prepare plans to cope with emergencies and also consider security of the premises and equipment,' I added, to make our purpose sound very formal. 'Oh, and this is Sergeant Blaketon, from Ashfordly.'

Blaketon held out his hand and Gordon shook it.

'Sergeant, this is Gordon Precious; he used to live in Aidensfield. He works for Ashfordly Rural District Council.'

'Pleased to meet you,' said Blaketon very formally.

I explained to Gordon, 'We saw the smoke and washing. I'd always thought the cottage was deserted, so I thought I'd better check. I'm always on the look-out for illegal campers, squatters, that sort of thing. I had no idea you were living here.'

'I am here quite legally.' He smiled briefly. 'But I'm pleased you came, it shows someone cares about such things. But my life has changed, I'm not with the council any more!'

I could sense the relief in his voice and demeanour, as I asked, 'Aren't you?'

'No, I resigned. I gave up my secure boring job and my pension so I could be an artist. We've been here almost a year, Deirdre and me that is.'

'I hadn't noticed you around Aidensfield recently and wondered if you'd changed your job,' I acknowledged. 'I've seen Deirdre in the Hopbind, but had no idea you'd moved to Ramsdale.'

'It's a dream come true. I'm a full-time artist at last ... I had a small legacy from an uncle to help me make up my mind, and that first exhibition sold out of my paintings, with lots of commissions to follow. This place, this new dam, has provided me with a lot of work, people wanting pictures of Ramsdale before and after the reservoir. It was almost a miracle that I got the chance to have this place; it's as if I was destined to have the house. Swanland offered it for a peppercorn rent because it needed quite a lot of work to make it habitable after being empty for so long. I heard about it through the council, so Deirdre and I sold our house in Aidensfield to generate more capital and that helped towards the upgrading. She's kept her part-time job at the shop in Ashfordly and at the Hopbind, so that helps to make ends meet while I establish myself. I've learned to drive but Deirdre usually takes the car to work and to her bar job at Elsinby. So here I am ...' and he spread his arms in a gesture of complete happiness and contentment.

'Gordon, I'm delighted. And are you happy here?'

'Utterly content and totally fulfilled!' he smiled. 'I've lots of work on hand. I've got a studio where I can work, and lots of outbuildings, one of which we can turn into a showroom where I'll put my finished paintings on show, those which are not commissioned. Our plans are to have that showroom ready when the visitors start coming to visit the new lake. I reckon they'll do that even during the construction process, long before the water begins to rise. Deirdre might even give up her work to run the place, we could even make teas and sell souvenirs, we've room for all that. Postcards, tourist booklets, that sort of thing. We've all sorts of plans. But right now, this is a small corner of our heaven, even though there'll be workmen and noisy machines just along the lane. But that won't last for ever. I'm thinking in the long term—my future is here.'

'I wish you every success,' and I meant every word.

'Come in, both of you,' he invited. 'I'll show you my studio. It's not often I get visitors. How about a coffee?'

'We'd love one,' beamed Sergeant Blaketon.

I must admit I had never seen Gordon so enthusiastic about anything and quite clearly, he was a new man; he was his own boss, earning a living from what he enjoyed and from what he was skilled at doing, and there were opportunities for the future, whether or not he found markets for his paintings. There was no doubt in my mind, and in his, that he had made the right decision. We followed him into his studio.

Gordon, clearly thrilled by his new life, brewed us a mug of coffee, showed us several unfinished works, many lacking the gloominess of his earlier efforts, and then he provided us with a guided tour of the spacious premises. Electricity and water had been installed, along with a bathroom, flush toilet and heating system, although I was pleased the open fires had been retained. Indeed, the one in the lounge was blazing with birch logs, but in general, the house was unspoilt with its stone kitchen floor and ceilings with ancient oak beams. Ramsdale House had lots of useful outbuildings and extensions, ideal for Gordon's future plans.

He told us that several outlets in Ashfordly and district, such as stationers, pubs and even a fruit shop, had agreed to display and sell his paintings on a commission basis and he regarded that as important. It meant he had a market for his work well away from home, in places regularly visited by the public.

I noticed one finished work which depicted Ramsdale Bridge in its present setting and asked for a price; having agreed to it, I reserved the painting and said I would call later with the money.

He did say he wanted to produce picture postcard-sized prints from this painting, recognizing its nostalgic effect. But we enjoyed the visit and were invited to pop in any time we were in the dale.

'The coffee pot will always be on,' smiled Gordon. 'I welcome visitors when I'm at home, but I'm not in the house all the time. I do get out; I've a lot of work in the open air and have several outdoor commissions to complete before the dale is flooded. It's surprising how many people want to remember Ramsdale as it is now.'

And so, with a feeling of contentment and perhaps a touch of envy, Sergeant Blaketon and I bade farewell to Gordon Precious and returned to our car. But even as we were opening the doors to climb aboard, we heard a clanking noise which was accompanied by the groaning sounds of a labouring, slow-moving and seemingly very ancient motor vehicle.

'It's coming along the lane from the upper dale,' Blaketon said. 'It sounds like an old rattle-trap to me, one that's on its last legs, or last wheels.'

I thought it sounded more like two dozen dustbins all being shaken while full of tin cans or perhaps a load of scrap iron being tipped on to another pile of scrap iron or even several old

40

tanks engaged in close combat, but above the ringing noise was the clangorous sound of a vehicle engine. Certainly it was not a healthy engine—it sounded as if it had bronchitis or lumbago or both because in addition to its continuous groaning it also had a croaking wheeze or two plus some worrying hissing sounds interspaced with several intermittent and rather loud explosive retorts. Intrigued by the oncoming clamour and not believing it was one of the construction vehicles, our mutual curiosity demanded we walk to the gate and inspect the oncoming mobile cacophony. To do so, Sergeant Blaketon peered along the lane from behind the security of a high stone wall.

'I don't believe this!' he cried. 'It's Greengrass!'

Bearing towards us was the battered old truck which Claude Jeremiah Greengrass described as his pick-up; it was casting wet mud and earth aside as it ploughed through the soft surface of the green track with its springs and chassis groaning and grumbling as it bore its burden down the dale. Blaketon decided to bring the oncoming noise to a halt so he stepped smartly from behind the wall and into the lane, raising his hand in the traffic cop's 'halt' mode. There was a shriek of brakes, some skidding of wheels and slithering of the vehicle, all accompanied by further banging noises and curses of disbelief from Greengrass, plus a bout of shrill barking from his scruffy lurcher, Alfred.

'What the hell do you think you're doing?' bellowed the shaken Greengrass, as he poked his head from the window to berate Blaketon. 'Jumping out like that ... it's suicidal, Blaketon, that's what it is, leaping in front of a moving vehicle like that. I could have knocked you for six ... mebbe I should have ...'

'It's one way of testing your brakes and observing your doubtful driving skills, Greengrass!' Sergeant Blaketon was quite unperturbed by Claude's anger. 'So what are you doing here?'

'What am I doing? I'm minding my own business, that's what I'm doing, which is more than can be said about you!'

Blaketon's next tactic was to stride purposefully to the rear of the pick-up where he inspected the load. I have no idea what he expected to find, but there was a petrol-driven cement mixer, some bags of concrete, a pile of sand, some flagstones, several old oil drums—all empty—some tools, including a pick-axe and mallet, and other assorted paraphernalia. Clearly, Greengrass had either been involved in, or was going to be involved in, some kind of building operation and this intrigued

Sergeant Blaketon.

'You've not got the contract for building the new dam, I hope,' was Blaketon's next attempt to have the situation explained to him. 'If you have I'll start making contingency plans to evacuate the entire area because no dam of yours would be safe enough to hold a bathful of water, let alone a Yorkshire dale-full ...'

'Now I might just have put in a successful bid,' chuckled Greengrass. 'I mean, I know this valley well, I'm a landowner up here ...'

'Land-owner? You?' chortled the sergeant.

'You might laugh, Blaketon, but I own forty acres up there, two fields and a small patch of moorland. Been in the Greengrass family for generations, they have, thanks to the foresight of my great grandad.'

'And now they're going to be flooded!' grinned Blaketon.

'No they're not!' retorted his old adversary. 'They'll be just above the water-line, thanks to great grandad's foresight. He allus reckoned they'd build a reservoir up here one of these days, he said the land was no good for owt else. So he bought them two fields, up there, on the slopes, and a bit of moorland above 'em. And now they're mine. My own bit of moor and it's rich with rare plants at the top

43

end—*gentiana nivalis* if you must know. That's how I got the water-level stopped from going that far up. Folks don't worry about farmland being drowned but they do worry about rare plants. And there's nowt rarer than mine, not hereabouts anyroad. You only find 'em in the Scottish Highlands, and then only a few ...'

'What's he talking about, Rhea?' asked Sergeant Blaketon.

'He's got some rare plants on his land, Sergeant, valuable enough to persuade the authorities to reconsider their plans.'

'He's talking gibberish, surely? A man like this couldn't change the course of a huge project like a new dam ...'

But now I knew he could—and that he had! It was now that I remembered that name—it was Greengrass! It was he who had fought the battle of the reservoir, the man known for flower power with his rare plants! Years ago, I had thought the name of the protester was most apt even if I couldn't recall it. At that time, the name of Greengrass had meant nothing to me because I did not know the fellow, consequently the connection had evaded me—until now. I'd never anticipated I'd inherit the fellow when I secured Aidensfield beat. But Greengrass, a champion of rare flowers!

'Well, to be honest, he's right, Sergeant,'

44

I had to say. 'There is a colony of extremely rare alpine gentians on his piece of land, it was in all the papers a few years ago. The only other known specimens are in the Highlands of Scotland. That's how the water-level was eventually determined.'

'That's right, Blaketon,' beamed Greengrass. 'Seasoned campaigner, that's me. Plants protected, walls built, caravan sites prepared ...'

'Caravan sites? Is that what all this rubbish is for, Greengrass?'

'Well, if you must know, Mister Nosy-Parker Policeman, I'm building a concrete platform for my caravan. That's before I make a site for lots more caravans, for holidaymakers and tourists.'

'Your caravan?' puzzled Blaketon.

'Aye, my temporary home. while I'm working on the dam.'

'You're working on the dam?'

'I am, part-time, like, in a consultancy role, as they say. Advising on flora and fauna which is at risk ... me, being the owner of the land bearing the *gentiana nivalis* and a successful campaigner for wild life. So I'm going to spend part of my time in a caravan up there, on my land, to keep an eye on things, then I'll turn one of my fields into a caravan site, with running water, toilets and things, for when the tourists want to come and stay and sail

45

their yachts. And before you ask, this road is a right of way to my property.'

'I don't believe this, Rhea,' muttered Sergeant Blaketon. 'How does a man like him get involved in an important project of this kind? And a caravan site? Who in the name of the Great Jehovah wants caravans blocking these narrow lanes? We've enough problems with traffic as it is, without him generating hold-ups with slow-moving mobile homes.'

'His family have been here a long time, Sergeant,' I tried to reason with him. 'He's lucky to have had an ancestor with a bit of foresight.'

'You'll have to be insured, Greengrass!' bellowed the sergeant.

'Insured? What for?' asked Claude.

'Towing caravans to your site ... you need special insurance.'

'I am insured,' Claude grinned. 'For towing all kinds of trailers, horse-boxes, sheep trailers, caravans, the lot. Now, if you don't mind, Sergeant Blaketon, some of us have important work to do. I must be off.'

And with no more ado, he closed the window of his pickup, rammed the vehicle into first gear and began to move forward. The resonant sounds resumed and continued as the old vehicle rattled and groaned slowly along the rough track as

46

Alfred barked his farewell. With a cloud of smoke from its exhaust, Claude's old truck disappeared from our sight beyond Ramsdale House but its departing noise lingered upon the cool fresh air.

'I thought this job was going to be a doddle,' muttered Blaketon, as he returned to the official car. 'I hadn't bargained for the Greengrass element.'

'Won't he need planning permission for his caravan site?' I suggested.

'Then I might just lodge an objection,' grinned Blaketon. 'On the grounds that visitors might damage his precious rare wild flowers.'

And thus we concluded our first official trip to Ramsdale.

In the weeks that followed, a clutch of prefabricated buildings appeared on the site near the pack-horse bridge in Ramsdale. Vehicles materialized, workmen in hard hats began to congregate and move around the area, private cars began to gather and a huge wooden sign erected upon tall legs near the entrance heralded the arrival of the main contractors. Standing close to the entrance to the site, the sign bore the name: Marchant French Civil Engineering Ltd.

This was followed by a Doncaster address and telephone number. A site office bore a smaller but similar sign on one of its outer walls and it was to that office that I went upon my first official visit to the site.

As huge, noisy earth-moving machines were clearing the massive area, I parked my motor cycle against the wall of the site office, tapped on the open door and walked in. I removed my motor-cycle crash helmet but the mild dry weather meant I had not donned my motor-cycle suit. Thus I was in my uniform which announced to everyone that I was a policeman. As I entered, I noticed, to the right, a small office containing a young woman working at a typewriter and another sitting at a high desk poring over sets of plans.

'Hello.' The typist noticed me and smiled. 'Can I help?'

'I'd like to speak to the site foreman, please, if he's available.'

'Ken Rigby, yes, that's his office to the left of the door, but he's over there.' She pointed in the general direction of some earth-moving activity. 'He's the one wearing a white safety helmet, it's got his name on.'

'Am I allowed to go over there while work's underway?' I asked.

'Yes, no problem at this stage, you could always wear your own motor-bike helmet if you're worried,' she smiled.

Replacing my helmet, I walked over the

muddy uneven ground towards the noisy, slow-moving machines and, eventually, a man noticed my approach. He waved to indicate he was aware of my presence, concluded his business with the driver of one of the machines, and began to walk towards me.

I waited in some awe at the huge scale of the operation currently underway, even though it was little more than shifting thousands of tons of earth, rock and undergrowth at this stage. Ramsdale Bridge and the old road were still intact. Soon, the white-helmeted man was within talking distance. He was smiling and relaxed, clad in what looked like a light blue boiler suit and steel-capped boots. I noticed that his helmet bore the name Rigby.

' 'Morning,' he greeted me, with his hand outstretched. 'Ken Rigby.'

'PC Rhea, Nick, the village constable from Aidensfield.' I shook his hand. 'This operation is on my patch so I thought I ought to introduce myself.'

'Good of you to come, Nick. Fancy a coffee?' He led me back to his office where the typist, Karen Richards, produced two mugs of coffee. With his helmet removed, he revealed a round, cheerful face with thinning brown hair and warm brown eyes In his mid-forties, his skin was weathered due to his outdoor work and he was of average height, not as tall as me but certainly wider. Stocky might be a way to describe him.

In the comparative peace of his office, Ken outlined the kind of work that would be undertaken over the coming months, beginning with what he called the unwatering. That meant blocking the route of the existing stream and diverting its flow so that the dam's foundations could be created. To completely rid the site of water was vital. He told me how the volume and type of work would change as the various phases were completed and how, in the longer term, water would gradually be reintroduced into the basin to form the new reservoir.

Even when the dam was finished, the reservoir would take many months to fill completely, with constant checks and counter checks of both the dam and the strata beneath the water as it was doing so. He showed me maps of the dale, sketch plans with and without the water in position, the routes of the new roads and access points, locations of key offices and power units, and everything he thought might interest or inform me.

In return, I explained how the local police had to strike a liaison with the contractors to determine a policy for dealing with emergencies which might include everything from suicides to sudden death by way of industrial accidents and sudden illnesses—but Ken knew the system. He'd worked previously on reservoirs, road construction, industrial complex building, earth removal—in fact, a whole range of large-scale operations. From his files, he produced some internal papers which he gave me; these contained all the information I was likely to require. We also discussed security of the site when it was unoccupied, and again this had been closely considered by Marchant French, as indeed it was with all their undertakings. He assured me they did employ their own security guards. I was provided with more papers detailing things like emergency telephone numbers, details of the security firm who had been instructed to protect the site at all times and the names of the key personnel. It was a worthwhile visit and, more importantly, I found Ken Rigby most friendly and co-operative. It was a good start to what promised to be a long working relationship.

As we concluded our coffees and our chat, I asked, 'So what role is Claude Jeremiah Greengrass going to play?'

'Who?' His brow furrowed as he puzzled over the name.

I explained the doubtful reputation of

our resident rogue, reminding Ken of the rare gentians on his patch of land and how he'd fought a campaign to save them.

'Oh, him; you mean the chap with the old army greatcoat and scruffy dog?' he smiled when my description identified Claude. 'We said he could be our flora and fauna consultant. It was to shut him up really, and keep him away from our workmen, and we said he could take rabbits from our land, so long as he does it while we're not operating. He offered to remove our waste for us—top soil, rocks, timber from felled trees, scrap metal and so on. But we have our own system of waste disposal, all carefully supervised—particularly for matters like oil and other noxious substances. So to keep him quiet, my boss came up with the consultancy idea and the rabbits. We don't want rabbits digging holes among our machinery, to be honest, so it does mean he'll be on site from time to time. And another chap who's been given almost total freedom of access is that artist in the farmhouse along the road. Our managing director has commissioned him to produce watercolours of our progress. We'll use them on our office walls and for future publicity.'

'He's called Gordon Precious,' I said.

'That's him, yes. A nice chap, bit on the quiet side but his work seems good if I'm any judge. Now, I don't think you'll have much trouble from our lads. Very few will actually live on the site. Some will be boarded in the village, Aidensfield that is, or even Ashfordly, at bed-and-breakfast places or even the local pubs. A lot will be bussed in on a daily basis although from time to time, we might have to resort to caravans for overnight accommodation, if there is a particular task to be completed by a deadline. But even so, the men will spend most of their time working, there'll be little time to spend in your pubs or chasing the female talent of the locality. But I'll try to keep you informed of such occasions, so you can make any necessary plans. I'll know of such things about a month in advance.'

'That'll be fine for us,' I said, and gave him the telephone number of Ashfordly Police Station, with Sergeant Blaketon's name should he need it. He introduced me to the two office girls, Karen Richards who was the site secretary, and Debbie Clark whose role was chiefly to ensure that everything that was needed in the office was ready and available, like the ongoing plans and copies of the contracts.

Both girls had found accommodation

in Aidensfield and would travel daily to the site, I was told; they'd rented a flat above the stores but would return home to Doncaster at weekends. Ken then told me that, being a single man, he had no settled home because of the nature of his work, and he practically lived out of suitcases. There was a bed in his office which he sometimes used, but generally he found accommodation in a pub. In this case, he was boarding most of the time at the Hopbind Inn at Elsinby, telling me that the reason for his choice was his interest in horse-racing. That pub was a centre for the local horse-racing fraternity, something he had already learned, and he'd discovered the tremendous rise of local interest in a horse called Western Cloud.

The owner lived nearby at Thackerston and Western Cloud had been entered for a race at Thirsk in the summer. Bets were already being placed by the locals—myself included, I'd risked £1 each way. I wished Ken well in his stay in the district and knew he'd be well fed and cared for by George Ward, the landlord. It was a very comfortable and well-run establishment.

In that way, I established my first important personal contact at the Ramsdale Reservoir project.

3

And, when once the young heart of a
   maiden is stolen,
The maiden herself will steal after it
   soon.
                    Thomas Moore (1779–1852)

One peculiarity about young girls who are
outwardly sensible and intelligent is that
some are attracted by the dubious charms
of scruffy, greasy, unwashed, itinerant,
uneducated and downright untrustworthy
young men. This feminine characteristic
greatly puzzles rational and honest young
fellows and so far as I know, none
has ever produced a satisfactory answer.
One Yorkshireman attempted to provide
a reason by saying aimless flies were always
attracted to muck, although he was not
polite enough to use to work 'muck'.

I must admit I wondered whether this
feminine trait would surface with the arrival
of the construction workers as it so often
did when travelling fairgrounds settled for
a few days. I did expect some dizzy young
girls would frequent the site in the hope of

captivating a crane controller or dazzling a dumper driver. I must admit, however, that the first few months were comparatively worry-free and that Sergeant Blaketon's doom-laden prophesies were not fulfilled. Apart from the occasional arrest of a drunk and disorderly dam worker on a Saturday night, or a summons for driving a car without an excise licence and insurance, or catching a tearaway roaring about on a battered old motor bike with a hole in the exhaust pipe, there was very little real bother. And no hordes of lovesick nymphs flocked to the site.

The outcome was that most of the fears expressed by local people did not materialize—and never would. None of the expected protectors or rent-a-mob turned up to make nuisances of themselves, no one vandalized the site buildings or stole any equipment, and there were no riots or random acts of violence by the workmen. Any real noise from the heavy vehicles was confined to the site, and even though some of them regularly passed through Aidensfield and neighbouring villages, I did not receive any complaints.

In time, however, one item of concern did materialize. The 'scruffy-man attraction' syndrome did manifest itself, albeit in a minor way. I became aware of it when two young Aidensfield girls were apparently being lured to the reservoir site. This arose through my own observations because no one mentioned the matter to me—certainly the girls' parents did not—and this suggested either that there was no cause for concern or that the parents were unaware of their daughters' destination. Perhaps I was being too diligent, but I did notice that the girls were enjoying rather more bicycle rides than hitherto. And I also noticed that those rides took them along the lanes and across the moor towards Ramsdale. Their motivation was, in my opinion, fairly obvious. I reckoned they were attracted to the rough, tough and virile site workers who would respond to their attentions, just as they would respond to any pretty young woman.

In this case, there was a particular problem: both girls were only fourteen years old and still at school.

In their casual outfits, however, each had the appearance of being at least sixteen, especially on those occasions when they tried to make themselves look older. Both were well-developed, quite tall girls who, with the right make-up and hair-style, would easily pass for sixteen or even seventeen. I think their fifteenth birthdays were not far away, probably in the autumn of that year, but that did not alter the fact that they were fourteen year olds.

They were Denise Emmott and her friend, Elaine Sowerby. Both families lived in the council houses along Thrush Lane, Aidensfield; the Emmotts at No. 10 and the Sowerbys at No. 12. They were from decent, caring families, Doug Emmott working on the railway and Frank Sowerby employed by the Urban District Council Highways Department. As both men were active in village affairs, I knew them quite well. Both enjoyed a night in the pub where they played darts or dominoes, both were proficient growers of vegetables in their allotments, while in the summer they were both keen cricketers.

Both played for Aidensfield and in this hobby they were well supported by their families. I'd often attended village cricket matches where I'd seen Denise and Elaine among the spectactors—although I suspect cricket might not have been the prime reason for their presence. Some fine young lads did play for the Aidensfield team and also for the opposing sides, and I had often witnessed the banter between them and these girls.

Denise had a younger sister and Elaine an elder brother; each of the mums worked part-time in the local school, helping with the dinners.

The families were friends and good

neighbours to one another, Denise and Elaine being playmates even before they started primary school. They had passed through Aidensfield Primary School together, and were now seniors at Strensford Secondary Modern, Denise considering hairdressing as her livelihood and Elaine contemplating a secretarial career.

As I became aware of the girls' increasingly frequent gravitations towards the reservoir site, I wondered whether or not their parents knew of their destination and their sudden interest in cycling and, if so, whether they would object. Girls, even those as young as fourteen who were riding bikes past whistling workmen, were not doing anything illegal, immoral or even dangerous, so was it any official concern of mine? It was one of those minor dilemmas which confront a diligent constable from time to time. Interference in contented family life is wrong; on the other hand, caring for families is right and justifiable, but where does one draw an acceptable dividing line? When a constable joins the Force, he or she swears to protect life and property, and to prevent crime, but in seeking to fulfil that pledge, where does unjustifiable interference begin?

I decided I needed more information about the girls' activities before I could determine my future action. If they were merely riding their bikes to observe the progress of the reservoir, then I should have no worries. But rather like their reason for visiting the cricket matches, I believed their real interest did not lie in a desire for knowledge of the building process. My worry was that one or other of the more irresponsible site workers might regard these nubile girls as available conquests.

In such an eventuality, there could be long-term problems for their families so the wise thing is to prevent trouble before it starts. I thought it might be necessary to alert their parents and in this, I had to bear in mind that there were very strict laws about sexual activities involving children under sixteen years of age. In reflecting upon this development, I decided my most discreet action would be to patrol around Ramsdale on those occasions I believed the girls would be there. In that way, I'd encounter them ostensibly during my routine work and with a bit of luck, I'd be able to decide if they were at risk. Whatever I learned would dictate my future actions.

Sometimes they rode their bikes towards Ramsdale after school, usually on a Friday evening, although on occasions they ventured out mid-week, apparently preferring Wednesdays. I wondered whether this was due to a light homework load or whether there was a particular attraction at the site on those evenings. They also rode towards the reservoir on Saturday afternoons and Sunday afternoons, the site being busy during all those times. Work never stopped except when it grew dark. Although members of the workforce did have their days off, these were staggered throughout the week so as not to interrupt the non-stop construction work. This meant there was always some kind of activity when the girls were haunting the place.

My low-profile strategy determined, therefore, it was early one Saturday afternoon when I saw the girls embarking on yet another of their outings towards the site. It was a warm June day, a highlight of which was to be a cricket match between Aidensfield and Elsinby.

It seemed the girls had decided not to be spectators on that occasion. The match would be played at John's Field which was the name of Elsinby's sports ground, and the fathers of both girls would be playing for Aidensfield. The match was to begin at 2.30 p.m. which meant the respective dads were conveniently occupied during the entire afternoon and well into the early evening which in turn meant they would not be around to ask searching questions of their daughters. The two mums had gone shopping to Strensford, something they did when the team played away from home. A home game, on the other hand, meant both wives voluntarily made teas for the teams.

With each set of parents usefully occupied, therefore, I noticed the two girls wheel their bikes into the village street. Each was clad in a pair of very short shorts, a bright T-shirt and sandshoes, with Denise tying her long, dark hair in a red ribbon behind, and Elaine allowing her blonde curls to be caressed by the mild moorland breeze. They mounted their cycles and, with some giggling and excitement, began to pedal towards Ramsdale, their interest in cricket and cricketers evaporating in favour of construction work and construction workers. I could envisage any red-blooded young man believing they were sixteen or even older. Certainly, they were highly attractive—and they knew it. I felt they'd outgrown any interest in schoolboys!

It was half past two as they passed the war memorial and turned towards the Anglican parish church, clearly making for the heathery heights which overlooked the village. The journey involved a couple of undulating miles across the moor and I reckoned it would take about half an hour because there were some steep ascents.

They'd have to walk up the hills and push their cycles to the summits, and there were very few downhill runs on the outward journey. I would therefore allow them one hour before I embarked upon a gentle patrol of Ramsdale on my official motor bike.

To occupy my time, I drove into Elsinby where I parked at the cricket ground to watch the game and chat with supporters. Aidensfield were fielding so I had no opportunity to talk with the girls' fathers, not that I had anything to say to them at that stage. No one commented upon the absence of Denise and Elaine, although I suspect one or two young spectators might have noticed their absence. Some of the players too, I'd guess.

In due course, I made my way to Ramsdale. It was a glorious summer day with the sun beating down so I removed my uniform jacket. I folded it somewhat ignominiously and stuffed it into one of my panniers. Thus I was motor cycling in my uniformed shirt sleeves albeit with my crash helmet in place. With the wild moors around me and a cooling breeze generated by my speed, I was thoroughly enjoying myself, even if this was classed as police duty.

When I arrived at the site, I saw the two cycles leaning against the stout wire perimeter fence but there was no sign of Denise and Elaine. The high, barbed wire-topped gate was standing open but there was no gateman or controller to deter trespassers. Inside was a sea of dried mud, all churned up with the activity of the heavy vehicles but hardened in the heat of the sun. Even so, there were some deep pools of muddy brown water and a good deal of soft soil around the site.

An earth-moving machine was operating —I could hear the drone of its engine and the sound of its shovel striking stone as it struggled to cope with huge buried boulders. There was a mobile crane too—I could see its lofty jib moving around as if picking a place to drop its grab. Perched on a tank-like base with caterpillar tracks, the big yellow crane was lifting huge iron water-pipes from a colossal pile and relaying them end to end in a long line which pointed down the dale. Their first use would be to carry water from the site during the unwatering process and, much later, they would be reutilized to carry any surplus from the outlets of the full reservoir.

Parking my motor bike close to the girls' cycles, I stood at the gate to survey the activity. I could see several helmeted men moving about, some on small dumper trucks, others on foot and

64

yet more operating what seemed to be a herd of earth-moving giants in the form of powerful diggers. But the girls were nowhere to be seen. I decided to pop into the site office in the hope I would find Ken Rigby, the site foreman. The secretaries who worked in his office were not there, being a Saturday, but inside I did find a man poring over a set of plans. He smiled and straightened up as I appeared in the doorway.

'Yes, Officer, can I help?' He would be in his late forties, balding, with rimless glasses, and he sounded like a professional man rather than a manual worker. This was the first time I had met him.

'I'm looking for Ken Rigby,' I said.

'Oh, it's his Saturday afternoon off, he's gone to Thirsk races. There's a local bus trip apparently, from Elsinby.'

'That's right. There's a well-fancied local horse running,' I told him. 'Western Cloud. Arnold Merryweather has laid on a bus trip from the pub. The whole village has put money on that horse!'

'Ken's gone with that trip. So, is there anything I can do for you, Constable? I'm Alan Haywood, the site engineer.'

After introducing myself, I explained I was making a patrol of the locality, something I did on a regular basis, and then added I had noticed the unattended girls' pedal cycles near the security fence. I explained the owners were a couple of fourteen-year-old girls.

'If they're on the site, they shouldn't be,' he said firmly. 'Come on, Mr Rhea, we'll have a walk around. I'll show you what we're doing at this stage, and if I find those girls, with or without any of our men, I'll send them packing.'

As he led me around the site, I noticed the absence of the little pack-horse bridge and the rustic lane which had crossed the dale. Both had vanished; as they had been within the confines of the security fences and behind the rows of huts, their removal had occurred without any outsiders realizing.

'Probably you know we're going to rebuild the old bridge,' Haywood told me as if reading my mind. 'We're going to resite it on the dam when the dam's complete, a kind of memento.'

'I knew about the reconstruction,' I smiled, 'but I didn't realize it was going to be a feature of the finished dam. I think that's a great idea.'

'It's our contribution to the local heritage, but not many members of the public seem to know about our plans. There's a place reserved for it on top of the dam where it will span the walkway. The public will be allowed access and it'll become an attractive feature. That was part of the agreement between Swanland Corporation and the estate but it never got into the papers. In fact, when the dam is complete, the whole project will be known as Ramsdale Bridge Reservoir.'

'That'll please a lot of people,' I nodded, not adding that I was one of those who was pleased.

'Right, now to find those girls,' he said with some determination. 'If they are on site, there's one place they're likely to be. Follow me.'

After plonking a safety helmet on his head, he left the office and strode with surprising speed across the muddy site, making use of specially laid wooden walkways where they existed, and I followed like an obedient poodle. Clearly experienced at negotiating muddy pools of water, massive heaps of baked earth and numerous lumps of twisted metal and discarded stone, Haywood led me to the mobile crane. As we approached, I could see the silhouette of the driver in his elevated cab, and could then distinguish two figures with him, one at either side. He was hoisting a huge black waterpipe into the air and twirling it around as if it was a matchstick, displaying superb skills to his captive audience. I'd heard it said that some crane drivers could lift an object as small and fragile as a hen's egg without cracking the shell or hoist a full mug of tea from the ground without spilling a drop.

All crane drivers were proud of their prowess and eager to impress their friends —especially girls—and this chap was no exception. He seemed inordinately skilled with huge lengths of iron piping, and I would not have doubted any tale which related to his abilities at those controls. He moved the massive jib around with astonishing precision, making it obey his commands with ease, almost as if it was an extension of his own arms. Haywood strode around to the front of the crane so that he was visible to the driver, then waved his hands and signalled for the crane's work to be halted. With a grinding of gears, the machine came to a halt, leaving a pipe suspended in mid-air. It began to move like a weather-vane in the wind, the crane's steel hawser acting as a fulcrum in the centre, but everyone ignored it. Quite obviously, these men knew the pipe would hang there quite safely for as long as necessary, swinging slowly in the soft breeze like a giant compass pointer. A sturdy young man in green overalls and wearing a yellow helmet over his long, dark hair clambered down from the crane and came across to us. He'd be in his late twenties or early thirties, I estimated, although the helmet made it difficult to determine his age. At the sight of my uniform, his face revealed some concern.

Haywood was very brusque with him. 'Who's that in your cab, Jeff?'

'Sorry, boss,' the driver was immediately contrite.

'Get them out, now,' ordered Haywood. 'Who are they?'

'A couple of birds from the village, I thought there'd be no harm showing them the crane, not today when it's quiet.'

'Do you know how old they are?' Haywood put to him.

'Old? No, I never asked. Sixteen, seventeen, something like that.'

'Fourteen,' said Haywood.

'Fourteen? Bloody hell!' I could see the driver was shocked by that information. 'Hey, with that copper here, you don't think ...'

'We don't think anything, Jeff, not yet. But you know we're not insured for unauthorized members of the public coming on site. Especially schoolchildren. I'm sure you don't want to do anything that would get the constable interested in your behaviour, either here or off site. They're gaol-bait, Jeff. So get rid of them and do it now. This is a warning: next time, you're fired.'

As the shaken crane driver strode slowly

back to break the news to his guests, I waited beside Alan Haywood. He said quietly to me, 'He won't want us to think he's kidnapping, Constable, but I've got to be extra firm with these blokes, otherwise they'll run all over me. In view of those kids' ages, he's lucky not to be sacked, but we need him right now. He's a good worker.'

I could understand his reaction but I was unable to take any official action unless he had physically interfered with the girls. So far as the site regulations were concerned, they were the responsibility of the contractors, not me. The driver returned to tell his passengers of this development and with lots of hand and head movements, he was telling them what had just transpired. After a short delay, the two sheepish girls climbed down from the huge crane and began to walk towards the exit of the site. Alan called them over.

'Here, you two, I want a word!'

Neither was wearing any kind of protective headgear, and they came towards us with looks of apprehension on their faces. I could see them looking first at me and then at Haywood. He spoke first.

'Who are you then?'

'Denise Emmott.'

'Elaine Sowerby.'

'From Aidensfield?'

'Yes,' they said together, trying to avoid looking at me.

'You could have got Jeff the sack, you know, coming on site like that.'

'Sorry,' they chorused.

'And you could have caused a serious accident, crowding into the cab of that crane. It's not made for passengers.'

'We didn't know,' said Elaine.

'Well, you know now. So I want no more visits like this, no more trespassing.'

'Yes,' they nodded.

'And I understand from the constable that you're schoolgirls, fourteen years old?'

Both girls were blushing now and lowering their heads; they were behaving like naughty children at this stage; gone was any pretence at teenage sophistication.

'I will pass your description around the site, to make sure my workmen keep you away from the place. So pass the word around among your pals: if one of our workers brings unauthorized people on to our site, they face the sack, immediately. No messing. They'll be out of a job before you can blink an eyelid.'

'Yes, sir,' said Denise, for them both.

'Right, I think you've learned a lesson. Now, does our work interest you?'

'Yes,' said Denise, wondering why this hard man had suddenly changed his tactics with such ease.

'Good, then if you want to see what's going on, you ask permission first. That's from either me or Mr Rigby in the site office, over there,' and he pointed. 'So the best thing to do is have a word with your form teacher and arrange a visit for all your classmates. You are senior girls, I believe? Then we can show you everything; we can make sure you are insured and we can provide the necessary safety head gear and so on. So, how about that?'

I knew this was not quite what the girls had expected nor did it embrace the real reason for their desire to visit the site, but it was a splendid piece of public relations work and I felt it would instil some kind of responsibility in the pair. They would respect Haywood for his adult treatment of them. Then, I took the opportunity to speak.

'Do your parents know you are here?' I looked at each in turn. They shook their heads.

'Shall I tell them or will you?' was my next question.

'Nothing happened,' spluttered Elaine. 'You know, nothing wrong, we just looked at the crane and had a ride in it.'

'Good,' I said.

I could see that they understood the deeper implications of my remarks, and then Denise piped up and said, 'I'll tell

72

my dad, about the school visit, I mean.'

'Right.' I addressed them seriously. 'Let's leave it at that for now. If you tell your parents, I won't, but I want to know when you've done so because I want to know their reaction. OK? So next time you come here, get permission. I think it would be a very good project for your class. Is that all right with you, Mr Haywood?'

'Sure, Constable. Fine. Right, you two. On your bikes and away you go. I'll have words with Jeff Asquith when you've gone.'

As the two girls walked back to their waiting cycles, Alan Haywood watched their departure. They moved across the site with all the sensual assurance of girls two or three years older.

'It's unbelievable, isn't it?' he smiled. 'Gaol-bait. That's what they are. A good description, Constable. Who'd believe those two were only fourteen?'

'Not your crane driver for one!' I laughed.

'He's had a fright, thanks to your uniform, but we do get girls coming to our sites,' he told me. 'Prostitutes sometimes, but other hopeful amateurs as well, camp followers really they are. I'll put a notice in the canteen, warning the lads about those kids.'

'I wouldn't describe them as camp

73

followers,' I said. 'Not yet, anyway. But that's what they could become if they continue like this.'

'Will you speak to the parents?' he asked, as he accompanied me back to my motor cycle.

'Indirectly,' I assured him. 'They ought to know about this little episode but I'll give the girls chance to do something themselves first. That'll show I trust them. But your invitation to the school was a good move.'

'We find it pays dividends in the long term, getting local groups to look around on an organized basis. I was genuine with my offer—I would welcome a school visit, or one from any formal group, male or female, young or old. We don't want local people to feel we're shutting them out, even if the sign on the gate says "no admittance"!'

By the time I returned to my motor cycle, Denise and Elaine were pedalling towards Aidensfield with never a backward look, but I did wonder whether this would be the last time they would unofficially visit Ramsdale or the reservoir site.

While I was in Ramsdale, I decided to visit Gordon Precious and to take up his earlier offer of a cup of tea. I'd have preferred a cool drink of orange or even lemonade but anything would help slake my thirst. When I eased the motor cycle into the paddock beside the house I could see Gordon in his garden. He had an easel erected and was painting a scene directly opposite his house. Calling out in advance, I went through the gate in the wall and he raised his hand to beckon me forward. I saw he was producing a watercolour of what looked like a ploughed field—it was in fact the base of the dale where the earth-moving machines had already cleared the topsoil as well as trees, dry-stone walls, boulders, scrubland and many other accoutrements of the countryside.

The enormous patch of bare earth now being cleared to facilitate the preliminary draining process would eventually become the bed of the new reservoir. It all looked like a gigantic building site but Gordon was being realistic—he was depicting the scene as a contemporary record for posterity with no attempt to conceal the reality. Beauty is in the eye of the beholder, I recalled, bringing to mind the words of the poet Margaret Wolfe Hungerford in her *Molly Bawn* and those of Lew Wallace in his *The Prince of India*.

'That's mighty good timing,' he said, and at my approach, he laid his brush in a tray beneath his easel. 'I'm about to knock off for a cool drink. Care to join me?'

'Thanks, Gordon, I'd love that.'

'Would you prefer tea or coffee?'

'Oh, no, something cool would be fine,' I said. 'I'm dehydrated!'

'Coming up in a few minutes,' he said, disappearing indoors. I admired his unfinished work, comparing it with the view opposite and marvelling at the way he had managed to catch the mood of this bleak scene. Soon, he reappeared with two long glasses full of pink-coloured milk shakes with blobs of ice-cream on top. Straws were poking from the froth, a welcoming sight. I maintain that milk shakes should always be sipped through straws. With obvious contentment, we settled down to enjoy the drinks, Gordon showing me to a stone bench in the shade of the house. As he acted as host, I realized that this was indeed a different Gordon. He was relaxed and self-assured, no longer an introverted character dedicated to standing at the bus stop in his dull brown suit.

'How's things?' I asked, after sampling my first delicious sips. 'I haven't seen you for ages.'

'Things are fine,' he enthused. 'I'm kept very busy and the commissions keep rolling in. I must admit I have the reservoir to thank for that; people keep asking me to produce paintings of the old scenes and the current scene and then they want me to do the new scene when the lake appears. That'll keep me going for years.'

'So long as you don't get sick of painting the reservoir,' I chided.

'I don't think I will. There's other work as well, so I do get out and about, over the moors and even across to the coast. But I must admit the bulk of my commissioned work comes from the scene right before our very eyes. There's been one good development, though: the contractors, Marchant French, have asked me to paint scenes of the development at the rate of one watercolour per month during the construction work. They want a series of water colours to hang in their head office, so you'll see me working on site sometimes—with a paint-brush and easel instead of a pick and shovel.'

We chatted like old friends although we were comparative strangers, and I told him the reason for my current visit to Ramsdale. I did mention the girls and he grinned. Although he had no children, he knew how young girls behaved when interesting men appeared on the scene, and then he told me he'd seen them once or twice, cycling in the countryside around the site or walking on the moors. In fact, he added, he had painted them into some of his pictures, featuring them as two anonymous girls on bicycles riding through the heather.

I told him about the projected incorporation of the old pack-horse bridge into the new dam and he expressed pleasure that the bridge would become a permanent feature of the dale, just as it had been in the past. Smiling, he said it would provide yet more material for his work!

In spite of our apparent friendliness, however, I did find him rather deep. I gained an impression that he was more eager to talk about his work than his private life and also thought he might be a difficult person to know intimately. I guessed that a close friendship with anyone would not appeal to him; he seemed to be happier on his own. But I had no wish to keep him from his work and so, once I had drained my milk shake with the inevitable noisy suction sounds from the straw, I thanked him for his hospitality, stood up and replaced my motor-cycle helmet.

'Is Deirdre working today?' I asked, by way of enquiring after her.

'No, she's gone to Thirsk Races,' he told me.

'I had no idea she was a racing fan!' I smiled.

'She's not,' he admitted. 'But there's a bus trip from the Hopbind at Elsinby. Apparently, there's a well-fancied local horse running in the three-fifteen, so the pub regulars have arranged a coach trip with Arnold Merryweather. Lunch at the racecourse followed by bags of betting and boozing with no worries about drinking and driving afterwards. Deirdre was invited so I told her she should go. She's been a tremendous support since I gave up my job to be an artist, she deserves a day out. I hope she comes home with a profit from that horse, though!'

'Western Cloud,' I told him the name of the horse so he could check the results. 'I couldn't go because I was on duty this afternoon. The horse's owner lives in Thackerston: he's one of the regulars at the Hopbind. I've a pound each way so I do have an interest in the outcome.'

In calling on Gordon, I had displayed an interest in his work and had offered the hand of friendship but I departed in the firm belief that he was totally content in his self-imposed lonely life. In some ways, I could envy him, although I was quite content with my own niche in society. We parted on good terms, with me saying I'd buy another of his works when I had sufficient funds, and he telling me I was welcome to drop in any time I was in Ramsdale.

As I chugged away from Ramsdale House, I wondered about the future role of this once peaceful dale, trying to anticipate just how the forthcoming changes would alter its former charms. In contemplating that scenario, I had a short time to patrol before I knocked off for my official break, so I decided to revisit the cricket match. I wondered how Aidensfield was faring and whether Western Cloud would romp home the winner at Thirsk Races.

4

Thou shalt not covet; but tradition
Approves all forms of competition
Arthur Hugh Clough (1819–1861)

I returned to the cricket field in time for the tea-break. Elsinby had scored a healthy 118 and after tea, it would be Aidensfield's turn to bat. During this welcome break, team members and spectators alike mingled with good humour, eating their ham or tomato sandwiches, home-made cakes and jellies while drinking gallons of orange juice in the bright sunshine. It was far too hot in the pavilion where the players and indeed most of the spectators would normally have eaten their teas, consequently everyone remained outside to enjoy the banter and inquests which inevitably enlivened this midway stage of the game. Slow reactions from fielders, dropped catches and contested decisions about lbws and runouts all came in for good-natured criticism.

Among the crowd, I noticed Claude Jeremiah Greengrass, not that anyone could miss him. He was neither playing nor spectating because he was serving lollies and ice-creams from Bob Clarkson's colourful van. With its serving hatch raised, it was parked just outside the entrance to the sports field where Claude, in a white overall, was doing a roaring trade. Alfred, his scruffy dog, was asleep underneath the van where it was cool and quiet.

'Now then, Claude.' I wandered across to greet him, wondering what devilment he was up to with the ice-cream. 'New business enterprise, is it?'

'The van belongs to my mate,' he grinned. 'Bob's gone to Thirsk Races with the rest of 'em from the pub, so I said I'd do business for him.'

'For a percentage of the profit, no doubt!' I chuckled.

'Folks like me can't afford to work for nowt, Constable,' he retorted. 'Business is business, even if you're helping an old mate out.'

'Well, I hope he shares his winnings with you as well,' I said, thinking I might indulge in one of his cornets when I had finished my sandwich and cup of tea. As I prepared to wander away from his van, I noticed the arrival of half-a-dozen young men, all strangers to this district. They had arrived in a couple of old cars from which they emerged with lots of banging doors and raucous laughter. With long hair, casual dress and a carefree attitude bolstered by repeated bouts of hilarity, they made their noisy way towards the entrance gate, then headed straight for the table from which ladies were serving refreshments. Then one of them noticed my presence in uniform and nudged his pals, whereupon they all became more subdued.

'Who's them lot?' Claude asked me, with slight apprehension in his voice.

'I've no idea.' I studied the men, wondering why they were here. 'But so long as they behave themselves, they're welcome.'

The newcomers bought plates of sandwiches and cakes, glasses of orange and then squatted on the grass to enjoy their meal, clearly intending to watch the second half of the game. It was while wandering among the spectators and chatting to them, that I noticed the arrival of Denise Emmott and Elaine Sowerby.

Leaning their bikes against the dry-stone

wall which bordered the sports field, they came through the gate, giggling to each other, then went to the refreshments table to buy plates of food. Eventually, they settled on the grass with some of their teenaged girl-friends and I could see, by the demeanour of all the girls, that they had discovered the presence of the six new arrivals. Observing people in such situations is always fascinating; it forms a large part of the life of any constable, whether on duty or not.

But there was no time to observe life's rich pageant or the ritual courtship display of the English male and female because it was time for the cricket match to resume. The two umpires in their white coats made their way on to the field and then it was the turn of the Aidensfield openers to stride out. Doug Emmott was one of them; heavily padded and carrying his bat with confidence, he made his way to the wicket accompanied by Jim Breckon. The small crowd produced a ripple of applause and it was then that one of the six newcomers came to speak with me.

'You're the local constable?' He looked me up and down, for I was not wearing a helmet or cap although I was clad in a uniform shirt. I'd left my crash helmet with the motor bike.

'Yes, I'm PC Rhea,' I said.

'I'm Andy Renshaw. We're working up at the reservoir, me and my mates over there. You'll know these folks here, most of them anyway?'

'Yes, I do,' I nodded.

'Which is the team captain? The Aidensfield team, I mean.'

'Stan Calvert. He's over there the fair haired chap standing next to the woman carrying that tray of empties. He's due to bat at number five.'

'Thanks, I want words with him. We'd like to fix a match between a contractor's eleven and the local village team.'

'Sounds a good idea to me.' I greeted the plan with enthusiasm. 'Anything to forge links between the village and the construction workers is a good idea. So talk to Stan about it, I think he'll be keen.'

I saw Andy Renshaw introduce himself to Stan, then they settled down on a bench for their discussion. I decided it was time to leave; I would enjoy one of Claude's ice-creams before departing, however, and I'd learn the result of the game in due course. I joined the small queue at the ice-cream van, and then noticed the distinctive black shape of Sergeant Blaketon's official car. It was being eased into a parking space outside the ground, and I could see the familiar figure of my sergeant at the wheel. Quickly, I detached myself from the ice-cream queue, hurried to my motor bike and located my cap in one of the panniers, managing to plonk it on my head before Blaketon found me. I did not worry about my jacket, however; shirt-sleeves were quite acceptable in these conditions. Besides, I reckoned my jacket would be extremely creased by this time. Suitably clad, therefore, I made myself conspicuous by walking towards the sergeant. I noticed that he was also in shirt-sleeves, a rare sign of relaxation for him.

'Good afternoon, Rhea,' he smiled. 'All correct?'

'Yes, all correct, Sergeant.' I produced the expected response.

'I thought I would find you here.'

'Did you call me on the radio, Sarge?'

'I couldn't raise you,' was all he said. 'I wanted to arrange this rendezvous.'

'I was in Ramsdale earlier this afternoon,' I told him. 'Reception's not very good in the deeper parts of the dale. I've just arrived here.'

'No problem.' He accepted my suggestion of being out of range, then said, 'Your wife suggested you might be here. It's a lovely day for a game of cricket on the village green, eh? And a happy crowd watching progress while the law looks on. An enduring picture of village life, I'd say.'

'I agree, Sarge. It's the quality of life that matters, and it can be found here.'

'So who's playing today?' was his next question.

'It's Aidensfield versus Elsinby,' I told him. 'A league match.'

'A local derby, eh? Good. Now, let's walk around the boundary,' he suggested. 'Then you can tell me about progress at the reservoir. No problems there, I take it? I trust you have established a working relationship with the contractors and work-force?'

And so we began our perambulation of the cricket-field boundary. Because of his interest in developments at the reservoir, I updated him on progress with the construction work, then switched to the cricket match that had just been proposed and rounded off that part of our discussion with this afternoon's invitation for organized groups to visit the site.

I told him about those because I regarded them as a means of showing that the developers did want to establish friendly relations with the community and that I was in touch with those responsible. I told him there had been surprisingly little crime and very few incidents of police interest; indeed, he was aware of all those because everything of that nature had been the subject of a report

86

from me. That was when he paused for a moment. By this time, we were at the far side of the cricket field, well away from the spectators. He stood in silence for a few seconds to watch the bowler release a fast ball towards Doug Emmott who dealt with it with consummate ease and sent it speeding towards the far boundary for four runs.

'Nice shot,' said Blaketon, wiping his brow with his handkerchief. 'Now to the purpose of my visit.'

He explained that an all-stations message had been received at Ashfordly Police Station this afternoon to the effect that there had been a nationwide epidemic of the theft of mobile cranes.

'Mobile cranes?' I almost shouted. 'Who on earth would steal something that size?'

'Somebody who wants a mobile crane in good working condition!' he grinned. 'Or somebody who has a ready market for them, either here or overseas.'

'But how on earth can you steal a mobile crane?' I asked. 'Surely the site security people would hear it being moved and besides, those things crawl along ... you'd hardly expect to have to stage a hot pursuit.'

'Don't ask me how they get the things away, Rhea. All I know is that someone is making a nuisance of themselves by nicking these things, and they're worth many thousands of pounds apiece. Nationwide, ten have disappeared without trace in the last eight months and we're asked to warn all building sites. We're asking them to make sure their cranes are secure when not in use ...'

'I'll search Greengrass's back yard, Sarge ...'

'You do, and make sure your reservoir site people lock up their cranes,' he said. 'I don't want any stolen cranes to appear on our quarterly statistics ...'

'Very good, Sergeant, message understood,' I smiled at him. I recalled some recent spectacular thefts—apart from the FA Cup, someone had stolen a whole streetful of door-knockers, other thieves had got away with a seven-ton footbridge, a steam-roller, a bath and toilet, an otter, a mystery-tour bus, a railway engine, a railway station sign for Llan fair pwll gwyn gyll go gery chwyrn drobwll llianty silio gogo goch and even someone's false teeth. People can and will pinch anything.

'And now,' he said, with all seriousness, 'I fancy an ice cream, something to cool me down. Come along, I'll treat you!'

He was in a remarkably good mood today, especially as he'd had to chase me all the way to Elsinby sports ground, and I thought the sunshine must be responsible.

But to offer to buy me an ice-cream—while we were in uniform? That was indeed a sign that he was very kindly disposed towards me at the moment. I hadn't the heart to tell him that the ice-cream salesman was none other than his old adversary, Claude Jeremiah Greengrass.

As we strolled around the boundary, there were cheers from the spectators as runs were scored by the Aidensfield batsmen but I had no idea of the current score. Judging from the cheers, Aidensfield were doing very well but I had no time to stand and stare because Sergeant Blaketon was leading me at a fast pace towards the ice-cream. There was no queue as I followed him to the little red and cream-coloured van. Claude was not in sight, probably he was having a sit down in the driver's seat and then I heard Blaketon rap on the counter and call, 'Service! Anyone there?'

There was a sighing and groaning noise from within, then the grizzled face of Claude Jeremiah Greengrass appeared at the hatch, having struggled from the front of the van. It was then I heard Blaketon shout, 'My God, not you, Greengrass! I wanted the ice-cream man.'

'I am the ice-cream, man, Blaketon, and I can be very choosy about my customers!'

'And I am choosy about my food. How do I know this stuff is genuine ice-cream and not some concoction which is contaminated with muck from years of Greengrass's unwashed hands?'

'Because I mix it with my feet, Blaketon, like treading grapes!' chuckled the old reprobate.

'I wouldn't be surprised at anything you do, Greengrass!'

'Give over, you daft bugger. This is all good stuff, Blaketon, fresh from the cows this morning and brewed to perfection by Bob Clarkson.'

'And who is Bob Clarkson? He doesn't sound like an Italian to me.'

'Look, do you want to buy one or are you just wasting my precious time?'

'Two cornets, please,' said Blaketon at last.

Claude lifted the metal lid from the cool canister which contained the ice-cream and then located the scoop which he kept beside him in a bowl of milky-coloured water. The water dish was on a counter, just inside the vehicle and within easy reach. As he was preparing to scoop out a portion for Blaketon, there was a lot of shouting behind us. For the briefest of moments, I ignored it, thinking it was the crowd cheering some more runs, but the sounds were those of alarm rather than encouragement. I turned just in time to see the cricket ball hurtling unerringly towards us as people shouted at us to duck or get out of the way.

'Sarge!' I shouted, pushing him aside.

But I was too late. As he staggered to one side, the oncoming ball just touched the side of his cap and knocked it from his head; ball and cap then flew inside the ice-cream van. The ball landed slap in the contents of the open canister, sending a spray of ice-cream in all directions while Blaketon's cap settled upside down in the dish of milky water in which the scoop usually reclined. I saw it sinking gracefully into the water.

'Six!' someone shouted behind us.

'Can we have our ball back?' called another voice, as team members began to run in our direction.

'What the hell's going on ...?' spluttered Blaketon as he recovered from the shock, clutching the side of the van to support himself.

'You nearly headed a cricket ball!' chuckled Greengrass. 'I reckon that skull of yours is hard enough to do that, Blaketon, but look what you've done to my ice-cream! And who wants a scoop that's contaminated with all those unidentifiable livestock that live in your cap ...'

'My cap's ruined!' shouted Blaketon,

reaching in to lift it from the basin. It was now coloured creamy white and contained half a bowl of the milky-coloured water. He tipped it on to the ground and shook it to get rid of the lingering drops, but made no attempt to replace it on his head. I wondered if it would remain discoloured for ever ...

'Is anybody hurt?' The Elsinby captain had reached us now and his face showed his anxiety.

'No, but my ice-cream's ruined!' moaned Greengrass, lifting out the ball with his ice-cream scoop.

'That's a fairish good portion,' grinned the cricketer.

'Aye, and we've replaced that little scoop with Sergeant Blaketon's cap, you get bigger portions like that. A cap full of ice-cream with a unique Brylcreem flavour. That's if you want to eat anything that's been in his cap. Now, anybody want to lick this clean?' and he handed the slippery white ball back to the captain.

'Change balls,' said the umpire, who was making his way towards us. 'And six runs because it flew over the boundary. Right, lads, back to your places.'

'What about my ice-cream?' cried Green-grass.

'And what about my cap?' called Sergeant Blaketon.

'It's all your fault, Blaketon!' snapped Greengrass. 'If you hadn't headed that ball into my ice-cream van, it would have hit the side and bounced back into play.'

'I didn't head it! My head never even touched it! I wouldn't be standing here if it had. It touched my cap, a minor deflection, that's all, and now that's ruined, water-logged with ice-cream swill. I'll have to submit a report to headquarters for a replacement.'

'And you can ask 'em for the cost of a refill for that canister!'

'You've another canister. That one was nearly empty anyway; the stuff at the bottom was melted, that's why it splashed all over and it's only water on my cap, you can't claim for that, even if it is milk-coloured.'

'If anyone has to pay, it's the cricket club,' I tried to intervene.

'No, Constable.' Claude held up a finger like a schoolteacher. 'I'm outside the field, they're not responsible for what happens to me when I'm outside the field.'

'But it was their ball that ruined your ice-cream!' snapped Blaketon. 'Not my cap!'

'It was your cap that deflected the ball into my ice-cream,' Claude stressed.

'Look,' I said, 'it's no good standing here arguing all day. Claude, have words with

93

Bob Clarkson about the tiny portion of ice-cream that's been rendered unsaleable, or else give it to Alfred and say nothing. I'm sure Alfred would enjoy a cool drink, he's panting like mad under this van. Then open the other canister because we'd like to be served. And Sergeant Blaketon will not sue you for the cost of a replacement hat; he'll let the chief constable issue him with a new one.'

'Sue me? Why should he sue me?'

'You left the bowl of contaminated water in a place where the cap could easily fall into it, and if the cap could easily fall into it, then so could other muck. Not that we will mention that to any of the health inspectors we might be talking to in the near future ...'

'Cornets or tubs?' he demanded.

'Tubs,' said Blaketon, thinking the heat of the day would melt the ice-cream in the cornets. 'Two tubs of your best, fresh ice-cream, Mr Greengrass.'

'That'll be a shilling,' said Claude, as he began to open the new canister.

'A shilling?' roared Blaketon. 'I thought we'd get discount because of the trouble we've been through ...'

'One shilling, Sergeant!' snapped Greengrass. 'No concessions for the police, that could be construed as bribery of a law-enforcement officer!'

94

With some reluctance, Sergeant Blaketon handed over his money as Alfred appeared from beneath the van. Panting heavily, he began to whine because he was thirsty, and so Claude said, 'Hang on a minute, old son, there's a cricket-ball-flavoured milk shake in here for you.' He placed a bowl of Blaketon-flavoured milky water before the dog. Alfred began to lap it up.

'If that dog dies, Blaketon, I'll sue you ...'

'I might just decide to check your dog licence next week, Greengrass!' retorted Blaketon, grinning to me as we turned away. But the arrival of another customer prevented Claude's response to that challenge.

Having enjoyed that exchange and an ice-cream at Blaketon's expense, I bade him farewell and went home for my mid-shift break; this evening, I would patrol the area and pay visits to all the pubs on my patch and tomorrow would return to the reservoir site to warn them about the vanishing mobile cranes.

There were eight public houses on my patch, the most popular being the Brewers Arms at Aidensfield and the Hopbind Inn at Elsinby. Saturday nights were always busy, but there was seldom any mayhem. The only trouble might spring from a temptation by some landlords to sell alcohol after the end of permitted hours, and some young people who constantly tried to buy alcohol whilst under the legal age for so doing. If drivers consumed too much alcohol, they were a menace in their cars but the presence of a uniformed constable in the pub car park was usually a good deterrent and a reason for calling a taxi to get home. I must stress that I had very little trouble from drink-and-drive merchants, even if this was before the introduction of the breathalyser. Sometimes there'd be a problem with simple drunkenness but often the inebriated culprit was a resident of the village and the most expeditious solution was to take him home and let him suffer beneath a rolling pin wielded by his wife. Quite often, that was far better punishment than any court could impose.

On that particular Saturday evening, therefore, I listened to the sports news to learn that Western Cloud had won the three-fifteen at Thirsk, romping home by two clear lengths. Some good money-making bets had been made by the regulars of the Hopbind Inn, I was sure, and I made a mental note to collect my modest win next time I was in Ashfordly. I reckon I'd won about £8, a week's wages for me at that time! Western Cloud's success meant there would be a massive party in the pub that night which in turn meant that celebrators might forget the rigid closing-time of 11 p.m. Looking sensibly at the situation, it might be wise for me not to patrol the village at that time. I decided to stage a diplomatic absence from Elsinby later that night. I would make my routine Saturday-night call but I would do so well before closing-time. Furthermore, I would let the landlord, George Ward, know that I would not return. Hopefully, a happy time would be had by all, and I had to trust there would be no complaints of noise or nuisance from the village residents.

It was around ten o'clock that evening when I arrived at the door of the Hopbind. Being a mild summer evening in June, it was not yet completely dark and lots of happy people were sitting outside or merely standing around talking and sipping their drinks. There was a good deal of noise inside, all human voices, but somehow amplified so that it sounded more like a boxing match at Earls Court than a celebratory event at a country pub. I pushed my way through the throng all of whom were good natured, and managed to reach the bar counter. When I did so, George spotted me.

'Evening, Nick,' he called above the din.

'Nice party, George,' I shouted back. 'And a good win for Western Cloud, eh?'

'Brilliant! We always knew he had it in him; folks in these parts have won a few quid by betting early. And how about the Elsinby cricket team? They beat Aidensfield by two runs! They're celebrating an' all, so it's a real party night for us!'

The nice thing about the winning cricket team celebrating in this way was that the losing team were also invited to the party, and so all the players, their spouses, family members and friends came along. The combination of cricketers and racegoers resulted in a very full pub, but it was an extremely congenial crowd. In spite of the bustle, I managed a quiet chat with George who assured me he could cope with any problems which might arise, and so I assured him I would not return to the Hopbind that evening. He smiled in quiet understanding, but promised there would be no trouble—there never was, he ran a very well-conducted house.

Having concluded our brief conversation, I walked through the bar to the rear door, this giving me an opportunity to see who was in the bar. I saw Deirdre Precious behind the counter and noticed she was talking to Ken Rigby. He was sitting on a bar stool and their conversation was intimate and jolly, even if it was constantly interrupted by customers wanting drinks. In addition, I noted the presence of the six lads who had arrived at the cricket match. They appeared to have made friends with some local youths and girls—Denise and Elaine were not in the pub, I noted with some relief—and when Andy Renshaw spotted me, he raised his hand in acknowledgement. I took it to mean he had managed to arrange a cricket match with one or more of the local village teams, a good outcome to his visit, I felt.

I went home and booked off duty, thinking it had been a happy but curious day, not quite typical of my work as the rural constable of Aidensfield. The following day, Sunday, I was scheduled to perform a 10 a.m. to 6 p.m. duty, a rare bonus because it meant I had the evening off. A full evening at home was to be treasured by a rural constable and I hoped the weather would remain fine and warm because I wanted to arrange a barbecue in the garden with Mary and the children.

Next morning, I was pleased to see the weather had held; it was as sunny and as warm as yesterday. One Sunday chore was yet another tour of the pubs, bearing in mind that young people were not at college or school on Sundays, and that lots of youngsters did tour the countryside on bikes or in cars or even on foot. It was only to be expected that they'd try to buy drinks in country pubs and it was equally to be expected that country constables would endeavour to deter them. Accordingly, I returned to the Hopbind Inn and arrived just before its noon opening-time. The parish church clock was showing three minutes to twelve and I was surprised to see a crowd on the forecourt. Among them was a gathering of young men in singlets, shorts and running shoes, all with large numerals pinned to their backs. Several were local lads but some were strangers and among them I noticed the six youngsters I'd seen at yesterday's cricket match. The number carriers were lined up as if they were about to begin a running race. Not knowing what was going on, I entered the pub to find rows of pint pots standing on the bar counter. They were all full to the brim and neatly arranged in a row at the front of the bar; the bar itself was deserted. As I strolled along the line of beer, George emerged from his private quarters.

'Something going on, George?' I asked.

'Some daft race,' he said. 'If I was you. I'd stand well clear of that bar ... you could get knocked over. They start when the church clock strikes twelve!'

As if on cue, I heard the booming sound of the clock on St Andrew's parish church in Elsinby and with no more ado, the door of the pub burst open and in dashed all the competitors from outside. They were followed by the crowd and as I stood back to observe events, each of the numbered men grabbed a pint of beer and literally threw it down his throat. I noticed that someone was recording this on a clipboard then, having downed one pint of beer, each man galloped out of the rear door, into the car-park and along the lane which led from the village.

'Where are they going, George?'

'Across the dale to Maddleskirk,' he said. 'There's two pubs there. They have to down a pint at the White Lion first, then along to the Dun Cow, and then run over to Crampton and do the same at that new pub, the Crown, then down to Briggsby for another at the Greyhound and back here for a final pint—and all before closing-time at 2 p.m. A round trip of twelve miles, fuelled by six pints apiece. All on foot, with no cycling, lifts in cars or lorries, or any mechanical transport. There are referees in all the pubs to see the pints are drained to the last drop, and marshals along the roads to make sure no one cadges a lift or uses mechanical transport.'

'Whose idea was this?' I asked, wondering if this was just an excuse for the contestants to get paralytic.

'Why?' There was a flash of concern on George's face. 'Is it illegal?'

'I don't think so,' he was relieved to hear me say. 'So long as they don't get drunk and incapable, and so long as they don't drive vehicles or ride bikes when they're tanked up. And if they keep off the public roads, so much the better.'

'Most of the course is across the fields or through the dale,' he said. 'Well off the beaten track. It was all arranged very quickly last night, with all the landlords agreeing to take part. It's a bit of fun and a bit of publicity for them.'

'Well, so long as it doesn't get out of hand.' I did experience some degree of caution but could see no reason to halt the race. So far as I was aware, they were not breaking any of the laws relating to alcoholic drinks—unless they got drunk. But six pints each, in two hours? I wondered ...

'So,' I repeated my earlier question, 'whose bright idea was this?'

'Some lads from the reservoir site were in, they dreamed it up.'

'So what's the outcome of all this, apart from bellies gurgling with beer and legs behaving like Pinocchio's without the string?'

'There's two teams, a Hopbind team and a reservoir team, ten men each. First man home scores twenty points, second nineteen, third eighteen and so on. When everybody's home, the points are added up and a winning team emerges. The one with the most points is the winner.'

'And what does the winning team get?' I asked.

'Free pints bought by members of the losing team,' he told me in all seriousness. 'And the opportunity for a return match the following Sunday.'

By the time I had elicited this information from George, every competitor had vanished from sight, heading for the next pint stop along the route. I decided it might be wise to stage another diplomatic absence and contemplated a patrol around the lonely wastes of Rannockdale where there was no pub. Should Sergeant Blaketon question my motives for patrolling such a quiet and unpopulated place, I could always claim I was deterring litter louts or keeping observation for sheep rustlers.

As I patrolled the moorlands of Rannockdale that Sunday afternoon, I realized there was more to do than worry about pint-filled runners. It was a busy day due to the seasonal influx of tourists and during that outing, I made sure I showed my uniform in strategic places. Those places included locations where thieves loitered to steal from parked cars, where silly people on picnics lit fires among the tinder-dry heather, where others parked in farmers' fields among the cattle and then left the gates open and where yet more were known to steal rocks and rare plants from the moors in a pathetic attempt to fashion their suburban rockeries. Sadly, many visitors are nothing more than vandals in the countryside.

Police patrols of the kind I was undertaking are of value in the prevention of all crime and acts of vandalism and it was around 5 p.m. when I decided to return to Aidensfield. I intended to perform an hour's foot patrol in the village before concluding my shift at 6 p.m. But even as I entered the main street, I was flagged down by a pretty young woman clad in white shorts, a blue T-shirt, sandals and little else. I knew her—she was Iris Burgess who lived with her parents and brother at High Rigg Cottage between Aidensfield and Elsinby. She worked in a solicitor's office in Ashfordly and would be around nineteen years old.

'Hello, Iris.' She was panting heavily as if she'd been running. 'What's the matter?'

'It's our Keith,' she gasped. 'I was coming to see you.'

I waited a few moments for her to regain her breath. Keith was her elder brother, a young man about twenty-two.

'What about him?' I asked, sensing some drama was about to unfold.

'He's missing.' She looked distraught.

'Missing? Since when?' was my next question.

'Since dinner-time.' In the moors, dinner-time was around midday. 'He went on the run from the Hopbind and hasn't come back.'

I groaned inwardly. He'd probably drunk himself into a stupor or he might have gone off with his mates, but I could not ignore her plea. I would begin a search for him—and the obvious place to start was his own home. Quite often, we received reports of people missing when in fact they were curled up in bed, snoozing in the potting shed or snoring on the toilet. A police search is invariably more thorough than one conducted by untrained people who tend to ignore wardrobes, lofts, greenhouses, outside buildings and hiding places under the bed or in the garden.

'Hop on to the pillion,' I told her. 'We'll start at your house.'

Tom and Hilda Burgess, both in their fifties, were in the garden when I arrived at their beautiful cottage. Dressed in a heavy frock with an apron over her knees, Hilda was sitting on a stool and shelling peas into a basin while her husband, Tom, with a handkerchief knotted over his head. was weeding a patch of his garden with a hoe. He wore dark tweed trousers, a thick, long-sleeved shirt and braces, his only concession to the hot day being that he wore no tie or collar, and his sleeves were rolled up.

'Now then Mr Rhea,' he said. 'It's a grand day.'

'Lovely,' I agreed. 'A bit on the warm side for gardening!'

'Nay, it's about right; it makes t'soil easy to weed, better than being sodden. Now, you'll have come about our Keith?'

'Iris says he's not come home.'

At this Hilda looked up. 'He never misses his Sunday dinner,' she said. 'He allus goes down to the Hopbind for a couple of pints of a Sunday, then gets home at quarter to one for his Yorkshire pudding and roast beef. Never misses. Regular as clockwork, he is.'

'But today, he has missed his dinner?' I wondered if he had come home and then gone out again.

'Nay, Mr Rhea, he's not missed his dinner, not yet. I've kept it for him, you see. He said he'd be late today, summat to do with going for a run, so we had to have our dinners and he said he'd get his after two o'clock. He said he'd get back to the Hopbind by two. I said I'd keep his dinner in t'oven; it's still there, Mr Rhea. Mind you, them Yorkshires'll be a bit on t'dry side and his roast taties'll have shrivelled up. It won't have done his peas much good either. But he hasn't missed it, not yet.'

'So what's he normally do after his Sunday dinner?'

'Goes to sleep in his chair. It's t'beer, I reckon. He comes in, has his dinner and sits in his chair then drops off. Stays there till tea-time, he does, snoozing happily.'

'Then what?' I asked.

'He has his tea, then goes down to the Hopbind for his evening drink, reckons it makes him sleep at night.'

'Do you mind if I look around?' I asked. 'His bedroom, toilet, lounge, outside places, just in case he's sneaked home without you knowing.'

'Well, we did have a good look around the spot, but help yourself. Iris, take Mr Rhea wherever he wants to go.'

With Iris as my escort, I made a meticulous search of the entire house, including the loft and outbuildings, but there was no sign of Keith. I noticed a telephone in the hall and asked Mrs

Burgess if I could ring the Hopbind, just to see if he had gone there, or if anyone had seen him. George told me that all the other runners had returned safely, with some in need of a drink even if they were a little weak-kneed. He added that the Hopbind team had won the contest in spite of a missing team member. They'd scored more points than the reservoir lads, which meant the reservoir lads had to buy them all a pint. That was due to be done tonight, so George told me. I didn't ask where—I was going to be off duty anyway.

'Any idea where Keith was seen last?' I asked George.

'The Greyhound at Briggsby,' he said. 'The umpire checked him in; he had his pint, knocking it back in a few seconds, and then set off for the last leg of the run, from Briggsby to Elsinby, across the fields. Two and a half miles or so. He was the last to leave, by the way, the others had all gone before he got there. He was puffing a bit, so the umpire said, a bit like a broken-winded gallower. He left in good time to get here before two, but he never made it. I didn't worry, I thought he must have packed it in and gone home.'

'He's never been home,' I told George. 'I'm ringing from his parents' home now, I've searched it high and low. He's not here. Anyway, don't worry at this stage,

George. I'll retrace his route from Briggsby to Elsinby, I can do most of it on the bike.'

'Do you want volunteers?' he asked. 'I could rustle up a few regulars to help you look for him.'

'Not at this stage, George, but thanks for the offer. If I don't find him during my local search, we'll have to consider something else and your lads could be very useful. Leave it with me for now, I'll be in touch later.'

The advantage of a motor cycle is that it can travel in places that motor cars cannot reach, particularly narrow footpaths and unsurfaced tracks. I knew that the cross-country route from Briggsby to Elsinby made use of a lot of green lanes, bridleways and public footpaths, most of which were accessible to my motor bike. I could very quickly check every inch of the route. There were several farms and cottages along the way too.

I could ask if the owners had seen a wandering or wobbly runner with a beery breath. If Keith had stumbled and broken a leg, or was in any other kind of physical trouble, I was confident I'd find him.

After explaining my plan to the Burgesses, I embarked upon my hunt. I decided to start at the Greyhound Inn, Briggsby, and work my way across country towards Elsinby. The first leg of the trip was uneventful; I chugged and bounced along the grass covered route without finding any sign of Keith. Eventually, I reached a gate, opened it, made a hair-raising trek around the edge of a wheat field, and regained the bridleway via another gate. This rough route took me towards Robson Hall Farm deep in the valley. Normally, I approached this farm from the opposite direction but was pleased to see signs of activity in the yard. The lady of the farm, Georgina Forster, was grooming a horse. The noise of my approaching motor bike startled the animal but Mrs Forster, a handsome, slim woman with beautiful black hair, held it in check as I brought my bike to a halt and switched off the engine. I sat astride the machine as she walked the horse towards me.

'Mr Rhea,' she smiled, holding the bridle as she continued to brush the smooth hide of the handsome animal. 'Are you on a cross country exercise or are you lost?'

I smiled at her. 'Neither,' I said. 'I'm looking for a young man who's vanished ... Keith Burgess. Maybe you know him?'

'Yes, I do know him. He's in my hay shed, fast asleep.'

'Is he?' The relief in my voice must have been evident to her, and so I explained the reason for my presence and for my apparently odd choice of route.

'He's not in trouble, is he?' she asked in due course.

'No, except from his mother. She might be rather angry that he didn't get home in time to have his Yorkshire pudding.'

'That explains it!' she chuckled. 'He came staggering into our yard dressed in running gear, a bit like a marathon runner at the end of his tether, and asked if he could sit down. Then he was sick all over the place, so I took him into the hayshed. It's dry in there and he sat on the hay, with his head in his hands. I went to find something to clean his clothes but when I got back he was muttering something pretty incoherent about being late for his Yorkshire pudding and then he slumped on to the hay and went to sleep. He's been sleeping ever since. I've been in to see him several times.'

I lifted the bike on to its rest and she took me into the hayshed where I saw the inert figure of Keith Burgess lying flat on his back with his vomit-stained vest and mud-stained legs.

'A fine sight!' I commented. 'He's doing this for fun, would you believe,' and I told her about the race in which he had taken part.

'He can stay there until he comes round,'

she said. 'He's not harming anything.'

'Thanks, now can I use your phone to tell his parents where he is? They're worried about him. I'll get them to collect him.'

The Burgess family were relieved when I announced Keith's whereabouts and Iris said she would drive across immediately. Then Mrs Burgess came on the line.

'Mr Rhea,' she said sternly, 'is our Keith capable of understanding things?'

'Not at this stage,' I had to admit. 'But when he wakes up, I'm sure he will understand whatever you say.'

'Just make sure he knows I haven't thrown his Yorkshire pudding out,' she said. 'There's no point in wasting good food, especially when he hasn't had his Sunday dinner so he'll have to eat it when he gets back, even if it is cold. And tell him the gravy's got a skin on it now.'

'I'll make sure he gets the message,' I promised, and Mrs Forster smiled her understanding. I thanked her for her tolerance, then departed for home with great anticipation of a quiet Sunday evening barbecue with my family. There would be burnt sausages, bacon like pieces of charred cardboard and scorched potatoes with raw innards—but I didn't think we'd bother with Yorkshire puddings.

5

His means of death, his obscure burial,
No trophy, sword, nor hatchment o'er
his bones,
No noble rite nor formal ostentation.
William Shakespeare (1564–1616)

The continuing development of the reservoir brought many benefits to the people and businesses of Aidensfield and district. Although some might be considered small benefits, they were consistent. The milkman, for example, delivered to the site and increased his income; the butcher supplied the canteen as did the baker, fruiterer and fish merchant. Other local shops and garages supplied groceries, newspapers, stationery, small tools, petrol and oil for the vehicles, electrical goods like bulbs and cables, lengths of cut timber and a host of other necessities.

One man who secured a very favourable contract was the Maddleskirk timber merchant, Paddy Stone. As the contractor's bulldozers toppled and uprooted trees and large shrubs during their landscape clearance, Paddy's army would move in, cut the trunks and branches into manageable lengths and remove them. He increased his work-force to cope with the extra work. In addition, all the local pubs, hotels and bed-and-breakfast accommodation did well from those workmen who opted to live in the district. They spent money during their leisure time too, patronizing a wide range of businesses from bookmakers to barbers by way of clothes shops, amusement arcades, cinemas and clubs. I was aware of these mutual benefits as I made my way to the reservoir on the Monday morning following the cricket match.

Upon my arrival, I found Ken Rigby in his office. Over a coffee, we chatted about Thirsk Races and the party which followed, not forgetting the running pints race and then I explained our concern over the thefts of mobile cranes. Ken was aware of the thefts and had already taken due precautions with his site equipment. He promised to contact me if any suspicious characters were noted near the site and already had a file containing the points of identification for his cranes.

I was about to leave when the door burst open and in rushed Claude Jeremiah Greengrass followed by Alfred, his dog. Upon catching sight of me, there was a curious mixture of surprise and relief on his face. I must admit I never expected Claude to make me feel welcome but this appeared to be one such occasion. He was out of breath and panting heavily as he lunged into Ken's office.

For a few minutes, he could not speak and so we waited with great expectation before he gasped, 'Over there, Constable, Ken, yon side ...' The effort made him fight for more breath. 'You've got to go ...'

'What is it, Claude?' I went closer and tried to calm him. Something had upset him deeply. 'What's happened?'

He fought for more breath, his old chest heaving with the effort and his brow drenched in sweat; even though it was a hot June day, he was wearing his old army coat and heavy boots. He must have been boiling inside that coat; certainly he smelled as if he was perspiring heavily. In fact, he smelt as if he'd been perspiring since birth! To say he smelled like a gorilla's armpit is perhaps an insult to the gorilla.

'A body,' he managed to gasp. 'Over there, under a tree ... dead. By, I'm glad I caught you, Constable. I heard your bike coming ...'

'A body?' I asked him. 'What sort of a body?'

'What sort of a body?' he glared at me. 'There's only one sort of body and that's when people are dead. It's a dead body.'

'Not a sheep?' I asked.

'I know a bloody sheep when I see one! Look, there's a dead human being over there, the other side of the dale, a skeleton in fact.'

'Skeleton?' I asked.

'Aye, all bones and things. I had the devil's own job stopping Alfred from carrying the chap's leg over here; he likes good bones and I think he wanted to bury it somewhere for dinner later.'

'So it's just a skeleton?' I put to him, anxious to clarify things before I set in motion the police procedures for dealing with a murder, suicide or sudden death. I had to know precisely what he had found. In some cases, bodies which appear to be dead may respond to lifesaving treatment if it is provided with sufficient speed, but if this was a skeleton, there was no such urgency.

'Aye, a skeleton, under a tree. That's what I said. Look, can't you come and have a look instead of just standing there asking daft questions?'

'All right. Show me. As this is on your site, you'd better come as well, Ken.'

'We'll take a site vehicle,' said Ken,

116

reaching towards the keyboard for a set of ignition keys.

In a small dumper truck, he conveyed us and Alfred across the muddy site as directed by Claude. He took us towards a larch which had been felled by one of the site-clearance machines. The shallow roots had been torn from the ground and the complete tree lay on its side, its branches crushed by its own weight. It looked a sad picture, this former handsome tree, but it was not particularly large and a bulldozer would have had no trouble pushing it to the ground.

'Stop here,' said Claude, and Ken obeyed. Alfred jumped out, tail wagging, as he loped into the hole left by the uprooted larch.

'Alfred, leave!' shouted Claude, clambering from the little vehicle. 'Leave, I say ...'

Alfred obeyed but he stood on the edge of the crater and whined, his tail wagging as he looked to his master for guidance.

'Leave.' Claude waved a finger at the dog, then said to us, 'Right, follow me. It's in that hole; I'll show you.'

When we reached the edge of the small crater, all I could see was a disturbed patch of earth which, at a casual glance, appeared to be full of broken roots and small stones. Alfred stood near Claude, his tail wagging

117

furiously as he whined and whimpered, apparently anxious to be allowed into the hole. Claude told him to 'stay' and stepped into the hole, gingerly making his way towards a collection of broken stones. He brushed aside some of the soil which had been disturbed even since he'd left the place, and at that stage, I could recognize a skull. It was the colour of the earth and looked like a chunk of ancient timber.

Having seen that, I could identify wood-like bones among the scattered stones.

'He's in here,' he said. 'Lying that way, feet towards where the tree is lying ... here, you can see his feet over there, and his ribs, and that's his leg; Alfred dropped it when I yelled at him ...'

'You were very observant, Claude, to notice those bones. Right, I agree with you it's a human skeleton, so we'll have to set our procedures in motion. I think he's been there a long time, though.'

'Do you? What makes you think that?' asked Ken Rigby.

'He was under the tree roots,' I pointed out. 'And that larch must be twenty or thirty years old. Nobody could have buried him under the tree—it's grown on top of him. Or her. I keep saying him, but it could be a female.'

'So what happens now?' asked Ken Rigby.

'We ask a forensic pathologist to examine the scene with the bones in place, then he'll remove them and have them tested in his laboratory. He'll be able to tell us how old they are. He might also be able to give us a cause of death, if there's a bullet hole in the skull or a broken bone in the neck, or he might find a broken leg. But if it's natural causes, or poison or something other than physical damage like a disease, then it'll be guesswork.'

'So we can't work on this part of the site today?' Ken asked.

'I'm afraid not, Ken. But the sooner I get my superiors informed, the sooner we get things moving and back to normal. Claude, I'll need a written statement from you as the person who found the body ...'

'It was Alfred who found it, not me,' he said quickly, not wishing to have his name in police records, whatever the reason.

'I can't interview a dog,' I said. 'So you'll have to act as his spokesman. It's just a few lines to record the event, that's all.'

'It doesn't make me a suspect, or owt, does it? You read of folks who find bodies being suspects for murder and, I mean, I never touched this chap. It was after Alfred had been scratching in that soil that I saw them bones ... we were rabbiting. We do

119

have an agreement, don't we, Ken? About rabbiting. Just in case the constabulary thinks I was poaching.'

'We do,' Ken confirmed, to put Claude at his ease.

'You're allowed to catch rabbits, not find bodies!' I laughed.

'It's no joke, I can tell you!' Claude muttered.

'Right. All I need is something very brief,' I said. 'I can do it now. I'll take your statement in my pocket book while we're waiting for the cavalry to arrive. Can I use your office and telephone, Ken? It'll save time, my motor-bike radio doesn't get very good reception in this dale.'

'Sure, no problem,' the helpful site foreman said.

'Right, let's go back to the office.' And so we clambered into the dumper truck with Alfred sitting on Claude's knee and were taken to Ken's office. He found chairs for Claude and me, then indicated the phone. I rang Sergeant Blaketon. I decided I'd give him a modest shock to start his week.

'Ah, Sergeant,' I said, as he answered my call. 'PC Rhea, I'm speaking from the reservoir site. We have a problem. There's a body here; it was found during excavations at the site ...'

'A body!' he cried. and I held the phone

away from my ear as he bellowed into it, 'You're not talking about murder, are you, Rhea? One of the site workers done another in during a fight, or something. Do we need to call CID?'

'I doubt it. It's a skeleton, and a very old one by the look of things,' and I then explained where it had been found and my theories about its age.

'Fair enough, no need to panic then. Who found it?'

'Alfred Greengrass,' I said, with tongue in cheek.

'Alfred Greengrass? Is that some relation of your resident rogue?'

'It's his dog,' I said. 'He was with Claude at the time.'

'Rhea, I don't like flippancy in matters as serious as found bodies! So what the devil was Greengrass doing on that site?'

'He's got permission to take rabbits, Sergeant, to clear the site in fact.'

'Well, tell him to stick to his job and not to go around finding skeletons. Right, I'll call the forensic lab and see if they can spare us a wizard this morning. And you'll need a doctor to certify death.'

'It is a skeleton, Sergeant, and it is very dead.'

'We must go through the established procedures, Rhea!'

'Very good, Sergeant,' I acquiesced.

121

'You need a doctor to certify the body is dead, and a forensic pathologist to establish the cause of that death, and then we must inform the coroner who might order an inquest. You know the routine, Rhea. Now, you stay there with Greengrass. Get a statement from him, not his dog! I'll ring the doctor and forensic, then I'll rendezvous with you there.'

'Right, Sergeant, I'll just ask about the best place to meet.'

'Beside the body, I would say,' he said, slamming down the phone.

I did not want to commandeer Ken Rigby's office because he would be busy; I was going to suggest we met in the canteen but Blaketon's blunt order was final. I explained this to the others. Ken graciously allowed me to remain in his office to take the statement from Claude, then we had another coffee before returning to the fallen larch. I found myself standing beside a hole in the ground with a skeleton to my right and Claude Jeremiah Greengrass to my left. Ken had remained in his office and Alfred was standing at the edge of the hole, whining from time to time and looking first at his master and then hopefully at the bones. In a strong voice, Claude told him to 'leave', and being a poacher's highly trained mate, Alfred obeyed. Sergeant Blaketon arrived very soon afterwards.

'Trust you to go poking your nose into things that don't concern you, Greengrass!' were his first words.

'I thought I'd give you summat to do, Blaketon! I wanted to brighten up the start to your week,' was Claude's retort. 'And if this chap turns out to have been murdered, then you're going to be very very busy, mark my words.'

'And if he has been murdered, you'll be prime suspect, seeing that you found the body!' returned Blaketon.

'Alfred found it, matey, not me,' responded Claude.

I wanted to stop this banter and asked, 'Is the doctor coming, Sergeant?'

'Doctor William Williams is on his way, he had one patient in his surgery and I explained there was a lack of urgency. And a Doctor England from the forensic lab at Harrogate will be here in about an hour. He'll decide whether we need call in the CID. Now, Rhea, show me this corpse or what's left of it.'

I indicated the various bones which were visible and knew the pathologist would carefully scrape away the earth to reveal the entire remains. I hoped he might make a speedy decision so we could determine our course of action. The chances were there would be no criminal investigation due to the age of the bones, and our only action would be to arrange their burial.

I referred Blaketon to my theory about the tree growing on top of the skeleton, and he said we might be able to determine the age of the tree, and thus have some idea how long the skeleton had lain beneath it. To cut short a long story, Doctor Williams went through the procedure of certifying the body dead and later, Doctor England examined it in considerable detail, saying the bones appeared to be very old, probably 200 years or more. An initial examination did not establish any obvious cause of death such as a bullet wound, fractured skull or broken neck vertebrae and it was his considered opinion that the person—he felt it was a male due to the shape of the pelvic bones—had died from natural causes.

Nonetheless, he would remove the skeleton along with samples of the earth which immediately surrounded it, and would endeavour to establish the age and sex of the bones in laboratory conditions. He might determine the cause of death—evidence of some poisons, for example, did linger in bones for years after death, and if there were any minute injuries to any of the surviving bones, he might be able to suggest their cause.

By the end of that day, therefore, the

bones had been removed to the laboratory in a large plastic bag and I thanked Ken Rigby for his assistance. He was then given the go-ahead to remove the larch and obliterate the grave of the unfortunate man as work on the site was resumed.

It was a few weeks later that Doctor England gave us his considered opinion. He said the bones were between 150 and 200 years old; they were those of a man aged around forty who was five feet six inches tall and who had had arthritic knees and wrists. There were strands of brown hair on the skull. The bones bore no sign of an injury which may have caused his death, nor were any of the known poisons found in his bones. In the doctor's opinion, the man had died from natural causes. As there was no evidence of a formal burial, the man might have died from exposure in a storm or possibly from a disease, although the remote location of the dale would favour the exposure theory.

There was no indication of his identity, no jewellery on the body like a ring or necklet, and his teeth were in surprisingly good condition, suggesting a sensible diet.

Doctor England advised us to inform the Press so that publicity might persuade a local historian to search old records in an attempt to determine whether anyone was known to be missing on these moors during the material time; It was not necessary to mount a suspicious death investigation and the CID could rest in peace, knowing they would not have an unsolved murder on their books, however ancient it might be.

Some time later, a local historian revealed that in the 1770s, a cork seller had vanished on those moors. He travelled around the moorland inns and farms, selling corks to the licensees and farmers' wives who then made and bottled their own ale and other concoctions. The cork seller, whose name was never given in the old reports, had vanished one January during a ferocious snowstorm. His body had never been found but the general consensus was that the Ramsdale bones were his mortal remains.

Disposal of the skeleton provided another example of the reservoir benefiting local tradesmen because the body was returned to the care of Maurice Merryman, the Ashfordly undertaker. He was charged with the task of arranging a suitable funeral, the costs of which were borne by the Rural District Council. Maurice arranged a quiet but decent burial in Aidensfield parish churchyard and the reservoir contractors paid for a simple memorial stone bearing these words from the work of Alexander Pope:

Thus let me live, unseen unknown,
Thus unlamented let me die,
Steal from the world, and not a stone
Tell where I lie.

Thanks to Marchant French, the unknown man did now have a stone which can be seen to this day. Even though he did not have a name, I always referred to the mystery man in later conversation as Johnny Corker.

I don't think the discovery of Johnny Corker's bones was responsible for the strange clause in the will of Warwick Humbert Ravenswood although, to be truthful, I shall never know.

Warwick was one of the characters of Aidensfield. A gaunt, gangly man, he was about six feet five inches tall and as thin as the proverbial rail. His head was egg shaped and the bald dome was adorned with a few wisps of unkempt white hair which fluttered loosely from the sides of his scalp, even in the most gentle of breezes. He looked like a flexible stem of decorative grass. I don't think he ever went to the hairdresser although I suspect he sometimes lopped pieces off his straggly hair with his own scissors. He wore tiny rounded spectacles over a spectacularly bulbous nose and had keen grey eyes which seemed to be restless and probing. He wore a brown leather suit too—the jacket was always buttoned tightly across his thin chest and his trousers seemed to be eternally crumpled—his suit looked most uncomfortable and yet it was always clean, as if he'd polished it thoroughly with his shoe brush.

One of my regular thoughts was that it should have been a motor-cycling outfit but in fact it was cut like a well-made lounge suit. I have never seen a suit like it, either before or since.

In his late seventies when I knew him, Warwick walked for miles around the village and moors, his slightly stooping frame and long, loose legs in brown leather trousers being a familiar sight to the residents. Quite often, he seemed to be striding nowhere in particular, heading across the moors in no specified direction but clearly enjoying the wide open spaces and the scent of the heather.

No one seemed quite sure of Warwick's background. Money did not seem to be a problem and he was never short of cash. He was unmarried and apparently had no close family, one persistent rumour being that his origins were aristocratic or even royal, but that those origins did not conform to the norms of acceptable society. In other words, people thought he was the illegitimate product of a high-born person and, in order to ward off any embarrassment to his ancestors, he was in receipt of a generous allowance. It was also said that a condition of that allowance was that he maintained the secret of his birth while living independently of his noble lineage.

I was never sure whether those rumours were based on truth, or whether they were the product of the imaginations of the villagers. Speculation about his origins probably arose because he did not work yet owned the splendidly situated Pasture House. A fine, spacious and well-kept stone detached house in its own grounds on the Elsinby side of Aidensfield, he had bought it for cash some years before I arrived as the local constable.

Pasture House was beautifully furnished with antiques and he employed a house-keeper although she did not live-in. She was Elsie Dobson, a widow who lived near the Anglican church at Aidensfield. She had looked after Warwick for years although there had never been any talk of a romance between them. There was also a gardener to tend the exterior and a part-time caretaker to keep the place in good repair. Warwick did not own a car, however, preferring to use public transport or to walk. He would sometimes walk the four miles into Ashfordly or the ten miles or so into Strensford to buy nothing more than a bread loaf or a daily newspaper. Walking was his life and he spent many hours alone on the moors. He seemed to cherish the atmosphere of total freedom offered by the unfenced moorland.

Well-spoken, articulate and full of charm, he was the perfect gentleman even if he was rather odd. Some of his ideas and behaviour were bizarre. In spite of the weather, for example, he would go salmon fishing in the river while dressed only in bathing trunks. He considered that to be very sensible because if he got soaked, it didn't matter, but the sight of his thin, white figure clad only in black trunks and waders did not seem quite right in the majesty of Yorkshire's only salmon river. One expected tweedy types in plus-fours and deer-stalkers.

Another of Warwick's foibles was to write long rambling letters to all the local papers and to Members of Parliament about current topics or to air his pet grumbles. He would also print posters on bright yellow paper which publicized his odd views and which he posted on local noticeboards.

He collected rounded green rocks from the beach at Strensford which he placed on a pile in the corner of his garden, the purpose of which puzzled everyone. He created a pond in another part of his garden to encourage frogs but it seemed to attract nothing but herons. He spent a lot of his time trying to build a pedal-operated machine which would fly and carry him from the cliffs at Strensford. Fortunately for him, that machine was never completed and it was kept in his garage, although it was sometimes rigorously tested in his garden, the rattling noise of its flapping portions alerting most of us to the fact that Warwick was still hoping to become airborne. Eccentric was perhaps an apt description of Warwick Humbert Ravenswood.

In spite of his peculiarities, everyone in Aidensfield liked him. He was quite harmless and in some ways endearing, but his *pièce de résistance* was the generosity he showed in the pub. He went to the Brewers Arms every Wednesday night for a drink and a snack, and again every Friday lunchtime for a cheese sandwich washed down with a whole bottle of red wine. Each time he went into the bar, he bought drinks for everyone who was there—visitors and local alike—provided they drank malt whisky. He would never buy any of the locals a pint of beer or a gin and tonic—without exception, it had to be malt whisky. No one ever discovered why he had such a penchant for buying other people malt whisky unless he had shares in a distillery. He drank it himself most of the time, albeit varying his intake with a single pint of beer on a Wednesday night and his Friday bottle of red wine—although he did drink malt whisky prior to having those drinks.

I am not sure how many bottles of whisky he managed to dispatch during the course of a week because he consumed most of it at home but I never ever saw him any the worse for drink in spite of his impressive intake.

Then one Tuesday morning in March, I received a telephone call from the postman, Gilbert Kingston. Based in Elsinby, his round included Aidensfield and he was the virtual eye and ears of both communities. This was an early call, it was not yet 8 a.m. and I was eating my breakfast. Fortunately, it was a duty day and I was scheduled to begin at 9 a.m.

' 'Morning, Nick,' he greeted me. 'I'm ringing from the kiosk in the village, Aidensfield village, that is. I think you'd better come, something's happened to Warwick.'

'Happened?' I asked.'How do you mean? What's happened?'

'I think he's dead,' responded the postman. 'I've called Doctor McGee and he said I should call you.'

'Has there been a break-in or something?' was my next question.

'Not that I can see, but he's lying on the floor in his sitting-room; I can see him through the window.'

'You've tried to get in? Is Mrs Dobson there?'

'No, not yet. The place is locked up and there's no sign of her. I've knocked and rattled the door; he's not responding.'

'I'll come straight away,' I said, reaching for my cap and telling Mary where I was going.

I arrived seconds ahead of Dr McGee and together we hurried to the window of the sitting-room where Gilbert indicated the still form of Warwick. He was lying on the floor, face down and spread-eagled with his hands over his head. I rattled the window and shouted but he did not respond, so I decided we must get into the house. I did consider trying to locate his housekeeper who would have a key, but felt it might be speedier if I broke in. A rapid examination showed an upstairs window was open. I found a ladder in the garden shed and it was the work of moments to prop it against the wall so I could lower the window and clamber into the house. I found myself on the landing, ran down stairs and entered the sitting-room. Before admitting the others, I felt his pulse—there was none and the body was cold. Poor old Warwick was beyond human help.

Then I admitted Gilbert and the doctor. Dr Archie McGee quickly confirmed Warwick's death, but said he could not certify the cause although it did appear to be natural, probably a heart attack. Together, we made a brief but thorough external examination for any wounds on Warwick's body but found none. There was no bleeding, bruising or broken limbs and nothing to remotely suggest he'd been attacked prior to death. Nonetheless, a postmortem examination would be necessary to establish the cause of Warwick's death and I found myself having to search the house for evidence of any other cause. I had to determine whether or not there had been an intruder or whether Warwick had committed suicide perhaps by taking an overdose of some kind, or if he'd left a note or whether he had simply collapsed and died.

Having explained to Gilbert that he was no longer required, I took a written statement while he was there—a few lines to record his discovery of the body—and then I released him. Likewise, I took a statement from the doctor in which he certified the death but reiterated his claim that he could not certify the cause, albeit with a paragraph to say he had carried out a brief external examination without finding any relevant wounds or bruising. Warwick was his patient but had been a very infrequent visitor to the surgery—the only prescription the doctor could recall was a course of sleeping tablets several years ago. Warwick had not been seen by him since then.

'Sleeping tablets?' I had to clarify the situation so far as they were concerned. Some suicides did attempt to kill themselves with barbiturates.

'If my memory serves me right,' the doctor frowned. 'I gave him a prescription for just the one course a long time ago, but the condition of the body does not suggest he has died from barbiturates. It looks like natural causes to me, Nick, but because he's not been to see me recently, I cannot certify the cause of his death.'

'I understand. I'll search the house to see if I can find any sleeping-tablet bottles, just in case.'

'You know your job. Right, I'll leave this with you. You'll do the necessary?' he asked me.

'Yes, no problem. And I'll notify the coroner.' Dealing with sudden deaths of this kind were very much a feature of my work. 'I'll arrange the postmortem if he orders one.'

'Undertaker?' he asked. 'Shall I tell him?'

'No thanks, Doctor, I'll do the lot, and I'll make sure his housekeeper knows. She might know how to trace his relatives, but the body will have to remain here for a while, at least until I'm satisfied no one else was involved, and that there was no break-in. I have to search for a suicide note too, just to prove there isn't one!'

And so the routine work of another sudden death was set in motion. It was quite clear to me the house was secure; there had not been a break-in, there were no damaged windows and no search of the house had been made. So far as I knew, nothing had been stolen. In the bathroom, I did find some sleeping pills but no sign of a discarded empty bottle. The date on the bottle showed they had been prescribed five years earlier by Dr McGee, and only half the bottle had been consumed.

I took the bottle and recorded my seizure of it, just in case the postmortem did reveal barbiturate poisoning, noting that dust on the bottle lid suggested it had not been opened for years. My chief aim at this moment was to search for a suicide note. Bedrooms, writing bureaux and kitchen tables were the usual places to find such notes but in spite of a careful search, I found nothing.

However, I did find a will. It was on the top of Warwick's writing bureau where it could not possibly be overlooked. There was a long buff envelope with the name W.H. Ravenswood on the front, followed by 'Last Will and Testament', and a hand-scribbled note saying 'To be opened in the event of my death'. I was unsure whether or not I was entitled to open that envelope, so I refrained and rang Sergeant Blaketon on Warwick's phone. I wanted to report the sudden death.

I outlined the procedures I had completed and assured my sergeant there was no suicide note. He said he would dispatch PC Ventress to Aidensfield to collect the body in the shell, the name we gave to the temporary coffin used for such events. Alf Ventress would set off immediately and would take Warwick's remains to the mortuary pending the coroner's decision about a postmortem. At this point, I mentioned the will I'd found.

'Leave it for the relatives,' said Sergeant Blaketon. 'I can't see it was meant for us.'

'I don't think there are any relatives,' I told him, following with an explanation of Warwick's odd life. 'But I'll leave it unopened for now. I'll go and see his housekeeper when I've dealt with the coroner and Alf; she might know how to trace his family.'

I was able to unlock the house from within, using the Yale lock on the front door. Within the hour, Alf Ventress arrived and we manhandled the long, thin corpse into the shell, after which Alf drove to Ashfordly mortuary. I telephoned the coroner from my own house and in view of the doctor's refusal to certify the cause of death, he ordered a postmortem. I rang Alf and asked him to fix a time, bearing in mind that I should have to be present for continuity of evidence. Having set in motion the necessary procedures, I secured the house and went to find Warwick's housekeeper, Mrs Dobson.

She was at home when I called, and invited me in.

'Is it right?' she asked as she made a pot of tea from the kettle on the hob. 'About Mr Ravenswood? They said in t'shop that t'police and doctor had been called by t'postman. There's a tale going round that he's passed away.'

'I'm afraid so,' I told her, not really surprised at the speed of the circulation of the village news. 'It looks like a heart attack, but there has to be a postmortem. It'll be later today, I would expect. Now, Mrs Dobson, you were probably closest to Mr Ravenswood, I need to trace his relatives and inform them.'

'There isn't any,' she said firmly.

'There's only him; his mother died a long while back.'

'Brothers and sisters? Cousins? Near relations?'

'None that'll own to having him,' she said. 'He told me that. He said when he died, we had to follow the directions of his will. He allus left it out ready, thinking he might die suddenly. It's on the bureau so as folks would find it easily. He told me what's in it, there's no secret, Mr Rhea. Most folks hereabouts know what he wanted when he died.'

'I saw the envelope,' I told her, 'but I thought I'd better not open it. I thought it would be for his family or his solicitor. I must admit I have no idea of its contents.'

'Well, you're fairly new in these parts. We all know, t'locals that is. Now, his solicitor is Benjamin Price of Price and Ridley, Ashfordly, but he made his will years ago and it's never changed. The contents of his house go to the Yorkshire Museum, his flying machine goes to an aircraft museum and the house has to be sold. I get summat, and so does his gardener and handyman, and the rest goes to charity.'

'He seems to have planned well in advance!' I muttered.

'He wasn't as daft as people thought he

was. Now, you'll want to know about his burial, I expect?'

'Well, yes. Once the coroner has released the body, I'll tell the undertaker.'

'Aye, well, Mr Ravenswood was very particular about the location of his grave. He wants to be buried in Ramsdale, Mr Rhea. Beside the beck below the pack-horse bridge, not in any graveyard. He was very firm about that. He wasn't a churchgoer, Mr Rhea, and reckoned nowt to spending eternity in a crowded churchyard. He said he couldn't abide having all them old folks around him for t'rest of his days and wanted to be buried in the quietest possible spot. That's why he chose Ramsdale, a spot of his very own near that old packhorse bridge.'

'Ramsdale?' I carried. 'But there's going to be a reservoir there!'

'He talked about that to me, Mr Rhea, and said he had no objection about being buried under t'watter. He allus reckoned he would die before they got t'reservoir finished so he picked his spot well. He made his will years ago, Mr Rhea, long before yon reservoir was ever thought of. He loved that old bridge and wanted to lie hard by it, he allus said.'

'But I can't see they'd allow him to be buried there now, not where the water will cover him ... I mean, people wouldn't want to drink water that had covered his remains ...'

'There's a lot worse things to be found in drinking watter, Mr Rhea, to say nowt of sheep droppings and dead rabbits ... and besides, he'd be in a coffin, well down in t'ground, I'd say, below t'watter mark. Anyroad, he allus did like folks to have a drink with him, and I'd say he'd give a right good flavour o' malt whisky to any watter that got into him. I hope there's not going to be a fuss about it: he was so very particular about where he was going to be buried. Anyroad, you chaps found a skeleton there, didn't you? That awd cork seller. I mean, if you hadn't found him, we'd have been drinking watter that had washed his bones and never thought no more about it. What's good for a cork seller's good enough for poor awd Warwick. One corpse down there's no worse than any other, and at least Warwick had a bath every day.'

It occurred to me that if Johnny Corker's bones had never been found, we should have happily drunk the water which would have covered him; we would never have known of or worried about his bony presence in our water supply. But if Warwick was buried at the bottom of the reservoir, I could see an enormous fuss being made. The problem was we'd all know that Warwick was flavouring our water. Even if his coffin was encased in concrete or lead and buried deep enough to be safe from the reservoir water, there would be vociferous objections. I could see that the interment of Warwick's mortal remains was going to be more troublesome than the disposal of noxious waste.

Later that day, I went to Ashfordly to attend the postmortem and it revealed that Warwick had died from natural causes, a savage heart attack.

The coroner authorized the release of his body so that the funeral could go ahead. Before contacting the undertaker, though, I popped into Price and Ridley's offices in Ashfordly and asked to speak to Benjamin Price. He was able to see me and I told him about Warwick's sudden death and explained what I had done so far, only referring to the matter of the funeral wishes once I had covered all the other points.

'He was very emphatic about the scene of his burial,' said Mr Price.

'But you can't just bury people where they want, can you?' I asked. 'I thought they had to be buried in consecrated ground?'

'Not everyone is a Christian, Mr Rhea, and there is no reason why people can't be buried in woods, fields or even in their own back garden, provided the necessary planning permission has been obtained.'

'Planning permission?' I must have sounded amazed.

'Yes, and Warwick did obtain the necessary permission before he died, a long time ago in fact. I have a copy in his personal file. It got overlooked in the deal when the land was sold—I think it will be interesting to see what transpires now. Warwick was quite happy for his mortal remains to be placed in something waterproof and weighted on the bottom of the reservoir, although that was not his original intention, of course. He wanted to lie beneath the sky, among the heather and with the wide open spaces of the moors around him. But he knew about burials at sea and felt that if he lived to see the reservoir full, then a burial-at-sea type of funeral might be available. But that is not necessary—there is no water in the place, so he can be buried in the ground long before the water rises to cover him. His chief desire was to be near the beck and close to Ramsdale Bridge.'

'But surely, there'll be objections from the public!' I stressed.

'I'll cross that bridge when I come to it,' and Benjamin Price chuckled at his own joke.

I realized, of course, that the funeral arrangements of the late Warwick Humbert

Ravenswood were not my concern; my duties ended with the issue of the coroner's pink form which authorized the handing over of his remains to the undertaker. Because Mr Price confirmed there were no relatives, I passed the pink form to him in his capacity as Mr Ravenswood's solicitor, and he said he would attend to the funeral arrangements.

Thanks to local gossip and speculation about the final resting place of Warwick Humbert Ravenswood, the local paper got hold of the story, and so did the nationals, radio stations and television newsrooms. The tale of the man who wanted to be buried in the reservoir was wonderful and it was during the time of that speculation that I paid one of my routine visits to the site. I found Ken Rigby in his site office and, as one might have expected, our conversation turned to Warwick Hubert Ravenswood.

'Oh, he came to see me several times,' said Ken. 'Marched in here with his leather suit and talked about his grave, wondering if he would occupy it before the water began to rise. Quite a character, wasn't he?'

'You've probably read the fuss in the papers,' I put to him.

'I have, but they haven't seen his will. Our contract solicitors tell me that its phraseology did leave a bit of leeway,' Ken told me. 'On one of Warwick's visits, I told him we were moving the old pack-horse bridge to a new location on top of the dam. He seemed relieved about that, pleased it was not going to be destroyed.'

'And did he mention the site of his grave?'

'Yes, he did. He told me his will says he wanted to be buried in Ramsdale close to the old pack-horse bridge and within sight of the beck. Most important, he said, was that his grave was close to the bridge. What we can do is to make a space for a grave without covering him with water. We can place him in the dam itself, in the front, away from the water and encased in local stone. Our architects have considered this and it's not difficult to amend their design. His grave would be directly below the old bridge at its new location and it would be overlooking the beck as Warwick wished.'

'Brilliant, but it'll take a long time. It means his funeral will have to be delayed.'

'That's no problem, he can be kept in a fridge until we're ready.'

'It might take three or four years,' I reminded him.

'So, no problem. Besides, the ice will keep his whisky cool!' laughed Ken. 'But we've talked about it and the mortuary will store his body for as long as necessary. My firm will pay the costs and we'll even pay to have an epitaph carved into the face of the dam!'

'Do his solicitors know about this?' I asked.

'Yes, I rang them and they've been to see me,' he said.

'Good, that'll prevent all the local specu-lation about Warwick-flavoured drinking water!'

I was to learn later that a large space would be reserved for Warwick in the front-facing reservoir wall, well above the water supply. It would be a tomb-shaped hole in the wall into which the coffin would be placed and it would be sited directly below the relocated Ramsdale Bridge. A memorial to his mysterious life would be inscribed on the face of the dam. It meant that Warwick would lie in peace hard-by his favourite old pack-horse bridge and overlooking Ramsdale Beck, just as he had wished.

His whisky-flavoured body and the water which would accumulate nearby were, in a rather odd way, a fitting reminder of the sad fate of the unknown man who sold bottle corks.

6

The man's desire is for the woman; but the woman's desire is rarely other than for the desire of the man.

Samuel Taylor Coleridge (1772–1834)

With the passing of the months, Phase I of the reservoir construction was completed. This had resulted in the removal of all water from the area which would accommodate the foundations of the dam and Ramsdale Beck being rerouted and piped away until its flow was required to fill the new reservoir. Phase II, the vital work of construction of the dam's foundations, could now commence.

During this preparatory work, relations between the construction workers and local residents continued to flourish. Apart from regular sporting events, dances were sometimes arranged for Saturday nights in selected village halls and Claude Jeremiah Greengrass had obtained a billiards table which he had installed in one of his outbuildings. I have no idea where he found it—to my knowledge, none had been reported stolen, and so it seemed a legitimate purchase. He arranged snooker and billiards contests and let it be known that his intention was eventually to transfer the table to his new caravan park beside the lake. He was even talking of arranging bingo sessions in a specially constructed hall at his proposed caravan park and had visited Gordon Precious to ask his advice about the procedures necessary to obtain a refreshment house licence from the council. Gordon, being an ex-employee of that council department, had obligingly given Claude the required information.

If granted, the licence would allow Claude to sell food and non-alcoholic drinks to the public from his premises beside the new lake—but that was a long-term dream without any current sign of reaching fruition.

From a police point of view, there was surprisingly little trouble at any of the joint events, even though it had taken some time for the feel-good factor to manifest itself. Most of the initial antagonism had evaporated with the local business community exploring possibilities of gaining benefit from the presence of the new lake. Swanland Corporation, however, had had the foresight to purchase most of the surrounding land and their attitude to the commercialization of the shoreline had not, at this stage, been revealed. Nonetheless, they did own land with enormous potential and entrepreneurs were actively seeking permission to rent sections of it.

Apart from Swanland Corporation, the only other person who now owned land along the shoreline was Claude Jeremiah Greengrass, and he was already formulating his own plans.

But there was one man who had not gained anything—not initially—from exploitation of the forthcoming reservoir. His name was Dave Jessup and for more than twenty years, he had been gamekeeper on the estate which had sold the land upon which the reservoir was being created. Although Ramsdale Estate had been gradually reduced in extent over the years through the sale of farms and parcels of moorland, it was the sale of Ramsdale itself which meant a full-time gamekeeper was no longer viable. With the arrival of the contractors, therefore, the unfortunate Dave lost his job.

I'd had very few dealings with Dave Jessup because most of Ramsdale Estate lay beyond the boundaries of my beat. The only portion on my patch was that which was now being turned into a reservoir. I did know Dave by sight, however, and we had met on one or two occasions, usually after receiving intelligence reports from York City Police, the West Riding of Yorkshire Constabulary or Middlesbrough Police that gangs of poachers were heading in our direction with dogs, vans and weapons ranging from pick-axe handles to shotguns.

At the age of 47, therefore, a rather shy and reserved bachelor with no skills other than keepering, Dave had been unable to find another suitable post. The estate had allowed him to continue the rent-free occupancy of his tied cottage either until he found work or until Easter next year, whichever came earlier. He also lost use of the estate's Landrover—a blow to someone living in such a remote area. The vehicle had been allocated to him for his work, but in spite of that loss, he was given permission to take rabbits, hares and other game which he could sell to earn himself a few pounds until he found a job. The estate did offer to find him casual work on its few remaining farms should the opportunity arise, but this was a very unreliable way of earning an income.

It was made clear, however, that the eventual intention of the estate owners was to sell Keeper's Cottage, thus Dave's occupancy was not permanent. Its address was Ewedale, a neighbouring valley. Located at the end of a long unsurfaced track some distance from the site of the dam, it was gloriously situated on the edge of the moor and it had a small paddock through which flowed a rock-strewn stream.

Access could be gained from the tarmac road which led from Aidensfield into Ramsdale and there was never any question of the cottage being submerged because it was in a neighbouring dale a mile or more from the reservoir. It was the sort of place that would appeal to anyone wishing to live in monastic solitude and it might have a future as a holiday cottage for romantically-minded townspeople.

When Dave lost his job, therefore, he had very little to occupy him. He spent much of his time wandering around Ramsdale watching progress at the reservoir and he was always accompanied by his border collie, Jess. As time went by, the pair became a familiar sight, both to me and the construction workers. Whenever I encountered Dave, I would stop for a chat and, although he was very reserved and quiet, he did seem to welcome news from Aidensfield and district. Although Aidensfield was a very short distance away, it was one of the places he seldom visited, his shyness perhaps being a factor. He wasn't the sort of man to venture into a pub alone or to strike up a conversation with a stranger. With no transport other than his two legs, he was very isolated in his idyllic moorland retreat and I gained the impression he had resigned himself to a life without a full-time job and without any close human companion. In spite of that, I never once heard him express any antagonism towards the contractors. He did not blame them for his plight—rather like the birds he had once cared for, he took each day as it came along, never looking back but always coping cheerfully with the uncertain future.

Then one morning, as I was patrolling Aidensfield on foot, I learned that Ted Fryer, the butcher's delivery man and van driver, had been rushed into hospital with a suspected heart attack. He'd been very fortunate because when he collapsed in the village street, his plight had been witnessed by the district nurse, Margot Horsefield. She had ministered to him until the ambulance arrived and he was now in the intensive care unit of Strensford District Hospital. Anxious to express my concern. I popped into the butcher's shop to convey my sorrow at the news; the butcher's wife, Sally Drake, was serving at the counter. In her mid-fifties with a happy, round face and cheerfully plump figure, she was clad in a blue and white striped apron and was busy slicing bacon for a lady customer.

152

'If it's Arthur you want, Mr Rhea, he's out with the van,' she told me as I strode into the shop to the jangling of the warning bell above the door. 'You've probably heard about Ted?'

'Yes, just now,' I said. 'I came to see how he was.'

Sally continued to slice the bacon as her customer waited patiently and said, 'He's pretty poorly by all accounts. It's going to be touch and go.'

'Does his wife know?' was my next question.

'Yes, she's at the hospital now, at his bedside,' Sally explained.

'So everything that can be done has been done?' I asked, wondering if I could be of any use to his family.

'Yes thanks. Margot was there when he collapsed, luckily; she was wonderful. Now, if you want to see Arthur, you'll have a long wait.'

'It's not important, not now,' I shrugged.

'Arthur's had to take the delivery van out—I don't suppose you know anybody who's looking for a driving job, Mr Rhea? You get about the place, you know what's going on ... it might not be permanent though.'

By this stage, she had weighed and wrapped the bacon for her customer, taken the money and rung it up in the till.

The customer left with a smile as Sally said, ' 'Bye, Mrs Dewhurst. See you next week.'

'What sort of job is it?' I asked. 'Is it just a case of driving the van and delivering, or is there some butchering to do?'

'Driving and delivering mainly. The meat's all cut up ready when it's loaded, although there might be a little bit of cutting up to do. Chopping chops, slicing beef, that sort of thing, but that's something any capable person can do with a sharp knife. You don't need to be a trained butcher to do it, in other words.'

'I'll keep my ears open,' I assured her.

'Don't make it sound too grand a job! If Ted recovers, he'll probably want it back because he's got a few years to go before he retires ... but there is a temporary job waiting for the right person, somebody who's trustworthy. They'll be handling cash, Mr Rhea, and meeting a lot of lonely women whose husbands are at work.'

I was about to say I couldn't think of anyone who was suitable when I remembered Dave Jessup. He could drive, and I was sure he was trustworthy with both money and women. I knew he'd welcome something to occupy him and I guessed he'd welcome a regular income.

Driving the butcher's delivery van might just suit him, and while on his rounds, it would enable him to meet people. That might help to conquer his shyness.

'Do you know Dave Jessup?' I asked her. 'The gamekeeper; he lost his job with the building of the reservoir.'

'A quiet man? Very shy and very decent, I'd say. Always dresses in plus fours and green tweeds? Works for Ramsdale Estate?'

'That's him. Well, he lost his job with the estate. They've sold so much land in recent years there's not enough left to keep him in work. He's out of a job, Sally. And he can drive.'

'I have met him once or twice; we've sometimes bought game from Ramsdale Estate. He sounds just what we need. Will you be seeing him?'

'I'll be visiting Ramsdale today. If he's in, I'll get him to call on you.'

'And I'll tell Arthur—he'll be pleased, he hates driving the van around the houses!'

Later that morning, I drove into Ramsdale and made time to visit Keeper's Cottage. I found Dave in his garden and he invited me in for a coffee. After chatting about the weather, the recent developments at the dam and some of the wild life he had watched that morning, I mentioned Ted Fryer and the van-driving job. I could see that Dave was interested so I advised him to visit Drake's Butchers as soon as he could—I qualified that

155

by saying he was expected, and that no butchering experience was required.

Dave smiled and assured me he did know a bit about gutting rabbits and hares, dressing game and poultry and even killing pigs. It was evident that dealing physically with strings of sausages and black puddings held no terrors for him, neither did cutting chops, slicing bacon or quartering poultry. He added he was due to visit Aidensfield that afternoon to do a spot of shopping for groceries—he'd been promised a lift in one of the dam contractor's vehicles which made a daily run to Aidensfield to collect provisions. He assured me he would contact the Drakes.

Dave Jessup was given the job and, very soon, we became accustomed to his cheery wave as he motored around the villages, visiting each in turn to sell from Drake's Butchers van. Tuesday mornings and Saturday mornings were his days for Aidensfield, with a weekly visit to Ashfordly market every Friday and to neighbouring villages on other days. After a couple of months, I chanced to see Arthur Drake and he was full of praise for Dave, saying he was a natural for the job and in spite of his quiet manner, had a wonderful way with the customers. All felt they could trust him and although Ted had been released from hospital, it seemed his heart condition was such that he would never return to work. He'd suffered a serious stroke while in hospital, and it had paralysed his right arm and right leg. It seemed Dave Jessup had a job for the rest of his life.

As I patrolled my beat, I would come across Dave touring his patch; sometimes, we would stop for a brief chat and he never lost an opportunity to thank me for putting his name forward, but I said the reason for his success was entirely due to him.

As time went by, however, I began to notice that the butcher's van would spend slightly more time than normal at a certain Aidensfield house. It was inevitable that, in time, this would produce some speculative gossip, as indeed it did.

The house in question was large and detached in spacious grounds and I knew the occupant well. She was called Eileen Bissett and she would be in her mid-forties. Usually, she was dressed in wellington boots and an old coat because she was invariably involved in work outside the house. She kept a veritable menagerie of animals and domestic fowl. To my knowledge she kept two horses, a donkey, several dogs and cats, some pet rabbits, guinea pigs, hamsters, ducks, hens and geese, and even a peacock. People took sick and injured birds and animals to her for treatment—in the short time I had been there, she'd dealt with several barn owls which had collided with cars and broken their wings, a Canada goose whose wing feathers had been clipped by vandals, a fox lamed by a snare, a badger that had gone blind and a peewit that had somehow lost a leg. I had dispatched several patients to her over the years, many the result of road accidents.

Her rough mode of dress tended to conceal her charms but she was a lovely woman with a fine figure and masses of blonde hair set off by a delightful and open personality. I had often wondered why she had never been tempted by a handsome man but wondered if it was something to do with the amount of livestock under her care, or perhaps because she had spent most of her younger days caring for her sick mother, now deceased.

The house was called Crag House, Aidensfield, and it had belonged to her parents, her late father being an industrialist specializing in chemicals whose fortune had been made on Teesside. Eileen, his only child, could live comfortably from her father's legacy.

I was to learn that it was her love of wild creatures which had led to her lengthy meetings with Dave. Someone had brought an injured but very tiny bird of prey to her for treatment and she'd been unable to identify it. Knowing of Dave's past work as a gamekeeper, she'd invited him into the outhouse which contained lots of wire cages and he'd identified the bird as a merlin. Thereafter he had popped in to help with the bird's progress and he'd shown a deep interest in the other creatures under her care. From those moments, there developed a romance.

I do not claim to be the first to identify the liaison as romantic, but I do know that Dave bought himself a small second-hand Ford which was sometimes parked outside Crag House at weekends and during the early evenings. On occasions, I noticed it on the moors, invariably empty as two distant figures strode through the heather or it might be parked at the riverside while Eileen and Dave took her dogs for a romp in the countryside. For a long time, each of them was very shy about being seen together in public. I must admit I did notice their shyness—if Dave happened to be working in the butchers shop and Eileen came in, she would blush a deep crimson and never talk to him; if they met in the street, they would smile and walk past each other coyly ... but to anyone with half an eye for the obvious, they were in love.

They were two very shy people experiencing the first flutterings of romance even if it had come rather late in their lives. Alone upon the spectacular heights of the moors, they could be happy with one another and safe from the passing crowds. That's when I'd often noticed them, hiking over the moors and through the heather in all weathers, two very happy people with a common interest.

And the inevitable happened—they decided to get married. The whole village turned out to wish them every happiness and Dave moved into Crag House, the first time he had ever lived in a village. He did not give up his delivery job, not wishing to give anyone the impression he had married Eileen for her money, but I do know they lived happily ever afterwards.

And so the reservoir opened a whole new world to Dave Jessup, even if it took a while for that bliss to materialize, and it also made Eileen a very happy and contented person.

But it was their romance which made me realize there was another romance which was blossoming right under our noses—and for a long time, none of us had noticed.

It is difficult to be sure when first I became aware of the flutterings of romance between Deirdre Precious and Ken Rigby. It began shortly after the arrival of the contractors in Ramsdale but I don't think Deirdre and Ken had met before then. Likewise, I don't think Ken's presence in the dale was the reason for Deirdre's ready consent to occupy the remote Ramsdale House, even if it was close to Ken's office. Furthermore, it was another coincidence that Ken obtained lodgings at the Hopbind Inn where Deirdre worked as a barmaid. In spite of these coincidences, I am positive the arrival of both Ken and Deirdre in Ramsdale, at around the same time, was not planned. but it did produce a drama which gradually unfolded before me. As I became increasingly aware of the couple's closeness, I began to wonder whether I was imagining or even fearing something deeper. Was their friendship platonic or was there some powerful sexual chemistry between them? Or was I reading too much into the moments I had seen them together?

On the occasions I had seen them with one another, the pair had always been within the public gaze. There was nothing furtive about their friendship and I'd never had any occasion to believe they were meeting one another in secret. In fact, it was practically impossible for them to avoid meeting each other at the Hopbind Inn. Ken slept in an upstairs room and had his breakfast and evening meal on the premises, the latter in the bar area when the place was busy. With Deirdre behind the bar, it was logical they would meet and chat. It was equally logical that, as the pub's most regular regulars, they would become friends. Likewise, Ken's work made it feasible they would meet in Ramsdale, perhaps while Deirdre was enjoying a walk or if Ken was taking a break from his daily toil. Because they were acquaintances, it was quite normal for them to stop and chat if they encountered one another in the remoteness of Ramsdale. They were two people whose circumstances had placed them in close proximity; that was a common enough occurrence among many men and women, one which was not guaranteed to lead to anything deeper.

I did realize, of course, that I knew very little about Ken Rigby's private life. I had no idea whether or not he had been married although I had never seen any photographs of children in his office. Men who worked away from home did take family mementos with them; Ken had not done so. Furthermore, I had noticed he did not leave the area at weekends, a fact which indicated he did not have anyone awaiting his homecoming. I did wonder if he had a settled home somewhere—perhaps he lived permanently out of suitcases, or did he have a small, empty flat to call his own? Another possibility was that he lived with his parents. In short, I had no idea of his personal circumstances but I had no intention of prying into his private life because that was nothing to do with me. Apart from my contact with him at his office, when he was always pleasant and helpful, I realized I knew nothing about him, except that he liked horse-racing. He couldn't have selected a more horsy inn as his temporary home and in the North Riding of Yorkshire there were lots of opportunities to enjoy the sport. There were courses at Thirsk, Catterick, Redcar and Thornaby, along with others nearby at Ripon, Wetherby, Beverley and York. Knowing so little about him, I wondered how much Deirdre knew.

In such cases, we can recall little things which were important but which, at the time, we dismissed as inconsequential. It was like that during the early months of their affair—looking back, for example, I had noticed that as they chattered in the bar of the Hopbind, their heads were often very close together and they would chortle at private jokes as they kept their companions from joining their closed world.

There were times Deirdre was unaware that a customer needed serving while Ken would suddenly realize his entire attention had been upon Deirdre to the exclusion

163

of others around him. I'd also noticed he openly blushed when someone made a reference to the way he gave Deirdre his undivided attention. In my visits to the pub, whether on duty or off, I had noticed all these things and more, but for many months I didn't pay any critical attention to what I was observing.

As the months passed, however, other circumstances began to materialize. Because I was a constable patrolling his patch at all hours of the day and night, I did become aware that Ken and Deirdre were indeed having a secret affair. My suspicions had been aroused by several apparently insignificant occurrences, such as seeing both in a café in Ashfordly or spotting them together in a car heading out of Elsinby, but first positive evidence came in the autumn. It was the Saturday of the September race-meeting at Catterick Bridge and I was one of the contingent of police officers detailed for racecourse duty. My first spell was in the car-park, always a frantic time as motorists whizzed in and expected to be shown into a space within the twinkling of an eye. Then, shortly before the first race, I had to move into Tattersall's for general uniformed patrol duties, keeping an eye open for pickpockets and other wrongdoers.

It was while standing on the steps of

the grandstand, admiring the tick-tack men and watching the crowds trying to decide where to place their bets for the 2.30, that I noticed Ken Rigby. He was standing in front of a bookie's pitch, poring over a list of runners.

I was on the point of approaching him when I noticed he had a woman companion—I hadn't seen her initially because she was standing a few yards away, one of the crowd. When he raised his eyes to check the latest betting, though, she went towards him and linked her arm through his. It was then that I realized it was Deirdre Precious.

Even at that stage I was not absolutely sure they were doing anything illicit, although I had no knowledge of an arranged outing to the races from the Hopbind Inn. From my elevated position on the steps of the stand, however, I had a clear view and it was obvious they were very close friends indeed. Deirdre was clinging to him like a limpet. I scanned the crowd for racegoers from the Elsinby area, but found none. Ken, with Deirdre hanging on to his arm, had an animated discussion with her, following which they went towards one of the bookies where Ken placed a bet. Then I lost them in the crowd—I think they went to the bar prior to the start of the race.

I never saw them again during that race-meeting and wondered if they'd noticed me in my uniform. If they had, would they want to keep out of my sight? I thought little more about it until the following Thursday. I undertook another of my patrols around Ramsdale, calling as usual at the site office where Karen produced a coffee. Ken was not around, he was meeting sub-contractors somewhere in the basin which would contain the new reservoir. I left without talking to him.

This meant I had time to visit Gordon.

I had a reason for this call because my parents had expressed interest in his work and I was thinking of buying a watercolour for their Christmas present. Gordon kept a stock for sale, so this visit, in the last quarter of the year, was opportune. He was indoors when I arrived, working in oils. This was a fairly new venture and he was standing before a large canvas depicting a moorland scene rich with the purple heather but imbued with the sombre darkness which was almost his trademark. There were times I wished he'd introduce more cheerfulness into his paintings. But this was not a reservoir scene and I got the impression he was pleased to be doing something different.

I watched for a few moments, marvelling at his ability to depict something as detailed as heather with little more than a few deft brushstrokes. He offered me a coffee but I declined, having recently enjoyed one in the site office, and I said I had no wish to disturb him at his work. He continued to paint as I stood at his side, and when I explained my requirements, he directed me to a small back room whose walls were full of his work, some framed and some not, some in watercolours and a few in oils but all depicting moorland scenes or the reservoir development.

I spent some time viewing them and eventually settled for an oil which showed Ralph's Cross among snow on the moors above Rosedale. He was asking £30 for it, not expensive in my opinion, and I returned to his studio to ask him to reserve it. I wanted Mary to see it before finalizing the purchase. As I entered, he was laying down his brushes, saying he wanted a break. Then he pressed me to join him for coffee. I did so.

Like two old friends, we talked about nothing in particular, our conversation ranging across his work and mine. Gordon laughed about his youthful exploits when rock-climbing and hiking in the Lake District and I responded with tales of mishaps with my succession of old cars. We discussed the reservoir, the moors in autumn, the reduction in tourists as the autumn deepened and the state of crime and vandalism in the country in general. In joining him, though, I had made a vow not to mention I'd seen Deirdre at Catterick Bridge races. I had no wish to stir up trouble between him and his wife—in fact, he might have been fully aware of her outing.

But suddenly, he started talking about Deirdre, praising her and expressing devotion and gratitude for her support in his endeavours to become an artist. I have no idea what prompted him to suddenly mention her but I could see the emotion in his eyes as he lauded her. Clearly, he worshipped her and, as his praise continued, I could see that, without her, he would not have abandoned his safe, dull job for his happy, but uncertain future. As he enthused about her, I did wonder whether he had a suspicion she was cheating him; it might explain his wish to defend her in this way.

'She's working longer hours now,' he told me. 'But I don't mind. I appreciate there's little to do in Ramsdale, and I like her to enjoy the extra cash. I'm earning enough to pay the rent now, and the household expenses, and I can keep myself in the materials. That's quite an item. Now that I'm earning on a fairly regular basis, though, it means Deirdre can afford nice clothes—she went to Harrogate with some friends last Saturday afternoon, looking at clothes. She didn't get anything but I'm happy that she feels able to do that.'

The significance of his words did not register at first, and it was only after I had left him to ride home for lunch that I realized Deirdre had lied to him about her outing last Saturday. She had not gone to Harrogate with friends, she'd gone to Catterick Bridge races with Ken Rigby. That she had lied to Gordon was an indication that her friendship with Ken was more than just a friendship. I was now faced with some kind of a dilemma—should I tell him what I suspected?

My years of police experience warned me that I should not tell him. I must not get involved. It was no business of mine. The couple were not committing any criminal offence and this was essentially a domestic matter. Much as I felt a deep sorrow for Gordon, much as I feared that his new world would crumble to dust in the very near future, I must not be the one to shatter his dream world. That must come from Deirdre, if indeed she would ever tell him. Maybe she would keep the affair a very close secret?

I left Gordon's picturesque home in something of a daze, my real concern being for him and his future. He had staked so much upon his new life and he had come to depend so much upon his wife. And now she was cheating him.

I told myself I had not caught them *in flagrante delicto*. My suspicions, I tried to argue with myself, were based on little more than a chance sighting at a race-meeting in full view of the public—plus a lie told by the lady in question. Had she some other reason for not telling Gordon she'd been racing? Was he against gambling, for example, or did he believe horse-racing was cruel? As I pondered these events, I found myself willing Deirdre not to do anything which would hurt Gordon.

I tried to make myself believe her actions were not adulterous, that whatever she was doing at the races was not hurting Gordon. But I knew I was being silly. I think it was during that ride along the peaceful and beautiful lanes of lower Ramsdale, that I recollected all those previous moments when I'd seen Deirdre and Ken together. His blushes, their physical closeness, the coach trip to Thirsk Races ... all done with people around. All innocent?

When Mary asked why I was dithering over my lunch, I deliberated whether or not to tell her. But if I did tell her, she would experience the problem of having to keep quiet about it and so I decided not to reveal names. I did, however, tell her of my discovery. I said I had very good reason to believe that a local woman was cheating her very nice and vulnerable husband, and asked Mary whether she thought I should alert him. Without flinching, she advised me against it.

'Nick, you come across a host of secrets in the course of your work, you must keep most of them to yourself. So don't get involved. Much as you feel some kind of responsibility to the husband, let them sort it out for themselves.'

It was wise advice and I accepted it.

A couple of nights later, I called at the Hopbind Inn and Deirdre was serving behind the bar as usual. The place was moderately full with a buzz of cheerful conversation, and I could see Ken at the far end of the counter. He was sitting with a plate of chicken and chips before him, tucking in with gusto. Deirdre was not talking to him on that occasion; instead, she was listening to a man telling her about his backache.

I entered the bar area, had a chat with George Ward, the licensee, and then caught Deirdre's eye. She saw me, waved cheerfully and grimaced as the backache man never halted in his lurid account of years of unyielding pain. Deirdre showed no sign of embarrassment so probably she had no idea I'd seen her with Ken at Catterick Bridge races. Maybe I was wrong about their relationship?

Several days later, though, I was walking through Elsinby while enjoying a foot patrol in the crisp autumn evening. I was working a late shift from 6 p.m. until 2 a.m. and had recently begun my patrol when I saw Deirdre's car easing to a halt just outside the Hopbind Inn. By the time it had halted, I was walking past; Deirdre emerged ready to begin work and I was surprised to see Gordon at the wheel.

'Evening, Nick,' she beamed, as she hurried across to the front door of the pub. 'Nice night.'

'Very pleasant,' I agreed, turning to talk to Gordon. 'You're acting as chauffeur tonight, Gordon, eh?'

'Deirdre usually drives herself to work,' he said, 'but Galtreford WI have asked me to give a talk about my work tonight, so I need the car. She'll get a lift home, she said, there's always someone she can ask at closing-time.'

Closing-time for the bar was at 11 p.m., although drinks could be served until midnight in the dining-room, there being a supper-hour extension in force at this inn. While I was chatting to Gordon, I told him Mary would like to view the

172

painting we had earlier discussed as a present for my parents, and he said we could pop in any time.

I explained I had two days off next week, Wednesday and Thursday, when I would endeavour to bring her. He suggested 11 a.m. was a good time. Having concluded our modest business, Gordon drove away to prepare for his talk and I continued my patrol.

It was just after 1 a.m. when I was completing the tour of my beat. I was on my little Francis Barnett motor cycle at that time and in the final hour had decided to undertake a late-night check on the perimeter fence which surrounded the dam workings. This was a routine task. Apart from the possibility that someone might steal a mobile crane, there were some valuable tools and vehicles within the compound, therefore a random police presence was not a bad thing. I chugged gently along the deserted road which led from Aidensfield into Ramsdale; it was pitch dark at the time, although the night was dry and rather mild for the time of year. In the far distance, I could see the glow from the night security lights of the site but knew that no one would be working at this hour.

I had done this patrol many times, always without finding anything or anyone suspicious but as I motored along the lane, I became aware of the glimmer of a reflection from the headlights of a parked car. It was concealed in the entrance to a copse of pine trees, well off the highway.

The lights were not burning but it was the glow from my own headlights which had been reflected from the car. If I stopped immediately, I would alert the people in the car and they would drive off—that's if they were there for an illegal purpose such as nicking cranes!

I drove on for a couple of hundred yards or so, then stopped, switched off the engine and dowsed my lights. I would investigate on foot; that enabled me to approach unseen and unheard.

Armed with a powerful torch which I did not switch on at this stage, I strode through the deep darkness towards the copse. I could see the outline of the pines silhouetted against the skyline and as my eyes grew accustomed to the lack of illumination, I could distinguish the shape of the car parked beneath them. There were no lights inside the vehicle and no one standing near it; if it was a car used by thieves, poachers or other villains, they might have left it here to go about their nefarious work on foot and in silence.

As I approached, I could see the car was a dark colour, navy blue by the look of it, and it was a Ford Consul. Even at this stage, I did not switch on my torch but as I drew ever closer, I realized it did contain someone. I could see movement inside ... the car was moving slightly and I caught sight of white flesh, male and female.

I switched on my torch and simultaneously opened the driver's door.

Two faces appeared above the seats, each blinking in the fierceness of my light. I had disturbed Ken Rigby and Deirdre Precious.

7

Absence from whom we love is worse
    than death,
And frustrate hope severer than despair.
William Cowper (1731–1800)

The embarrassment to Deirdre and Ken (and, I might add myself) did result in their eventual dissociation. In the heat of that moment, though, and as the car door stood open to admit the cool night air, I apologized for disturbing them but at the same time gabbled I was merely doing my duty. I explained, as well as

I could in the circumstances, that I had to check all suspicious vehicles seen near the construction site during early hours of any morning, particularly in light of the nationwide epidemic of mobile crane thefts. However, I did refrain from asking if they'd noticed any jibs or low-loaders.

If Ken had been fully dressed, I'm sure he would have leapt out to punch me on the nose, perhaps not realizing it was a police officer or me in particular, but the fact he was completely naked and lying in a rather peculiar position did restrain any attempt to physically vent his anger. He simply blinked into the glare of my torch as he strove to shield his vulnerable parts and at the same time protect and conceal Deirdre. Deirdre, as women often do in such cases, tried to cover her face while leaving everything else exposed and I think the chilly draught from the open door produced sets of goosepimples in some rather curious places. I am never quite sure what happens to the gear lever in such circumstances, whether shoes are always discarded or why the rear-view mirror is always covered.

After those first embarrassing seconds, I concluded with, 'I think it's time you went home to Gordon, Deirdre,' then closed the car door. I switched off my torch and quickly walked away.

Leaving them in the gloom to consider their more immediate future, I returned to my motor cycle which was concealed further along the road and sat astride it for a few minutes, awaiting their reaction. Several minutes ticked by and then, having had time to recover their clothes, get dressed, calm themselves down and decide their next move, Ken's car motored slowly towards Deirdre's home, but they did not see me hidden in my dark place. As I watched their departure, I wondered what Deirdre would tell Gordon—I guessed it would be to the effect that the Hopbind had hosted a dinner party which had lasted longer than expected. And Gordon, loving his wife so dearly, would accept her story. At this time of the morning—around 1.30—he'd probably be asleep anyway.

It was several days later when I had to call at the site office for a chat with Ken Rigby. There'd been another mobile crane theft, this time the thieves spiriting a monster machine away from a motorway construction site in the Midlands. It seems they'd used a low-loader, but what on earth did they do with the cranes? I had come to remind Ken of that theft and Karen welcomed me with an offer of coffee as Debbie went to tell Ken I had arrived. He was working on site; from the large rear window of the office, I watched

Debbie approach him. There was a brief conversation and then he waved to indicate I should join him. Karen presented me with two mugs of coffee and I carried them to where Ken was waiting.

We were totally alone, the only presence being an earth-moving machine operating nearby and drowning any conversation which might be overheard. But we could converse in raised voices. I presented him with one of the mugs before raising my own and saying, 'Cheers' in a show of comradeship. The expression on his face suggested he was relieved to see me.

'About the other night ...' he began, his face revealing his anxiety to explain.

'Ken, it's nothing to do with me,' I interrupted. 'What you do in your spare time is of no consequence to me, unless you break the law. And it's not a criminal offence to make love to another man's wife.'

'But I do owe you some kind of explanation. I've been wanting to talk to you, to explain. I know it was wrong ... it just happened ... we went too far ... but we've agreed to stop seeing each other,' he said quickly. 'I wanted you to know.'

'That's probably a wise decision.' Although it was no concern of mine, I felt I had to make a positive response.

'Deirdre cried that night, she was desperately worried about Gordon, wondering what he would do if he found out. I think he's vulnerable to black moods, depression even, and he trusts her totally. He depends on her more than we realize. She was ashamed of what we'd done.'

'Or ashamed she'd been caught?' I put to him, immediately wishing I hadn't said that.

'Both,' he said quietly. 'But it was she who suggested we part.'

'A wise decision, but I've not told anyone about you,' I assured him. 'It is not recorded in any of my official logs, and so far as I am concerned, there is nothing further to say about it. Most certainly, I have not told Gordon and I never will. That's between Deirdre and him, no one else.'

'She was all for giving up her job at the Hopbind,' he said.

'That's hardly necessary,' I responded.

'She couldn't work there if I was living in, so I said I'd move out. It was my fault, Nick; I made all the moves; I chased her. It's my responsibility. I know she loves Gordon and wants to support him. It's more than the money and I'd hate to ruin their marriage—it was a fling really, but you never think things will go that far, do you?'

'You're talking sense, Ken. Gordon does need her.'

'I know. In hindsight, I feel a right bastard. Anyway, I told her not to give up work on my account. So I'll keep out of her way. It'll be hard, I know, because, would you believe, that over the months, I've come to love that woman, I really have. She is more to me than just a bit on the side.'

'You're not leaving the site, are you?' I asked.

'Oh, no. I'll find some other digs, perhaps in Ashfordly or another village. I like pubs; they provide me with different company after work. I don't like living and working with my mates. Meanwhile, I've found a caravan.'

'A caravan? At this time of year! It'll be a bit on the chilly side!'

'It's on Claude Jeremiah Greengrass's site, that old crate of his. It'll do temporarily. I should be out before the worst of the winter. Maybe if you know of any good digs, you'd let me know? Those I've tried are full just now, catering for the last of the summer visitors.'

'Yes, I'll keep my ears and eyes open for you.'

There was a momentary lull in our conversation before he continued, 'I do know we attracted comments from the pub regulars, me and Deirdre, and I suspect George Ward was keeping a close eye on her. She is a good barmaid, reliable and trustworthy. Maybe we weren't as discreet as we should have been. You never think folks are watching and taking things in.'

'Gordon would have found out if you'd continued. But perhaps now he'll never know. It is all over, isn't it?' I put to him. 'Really over, I mean.'

He nodded and I could see the beginnings of a tear in his eye; he might have said it was due to the chill wind which was blasting across the site but I felt otherwise. I did wonder, even then, whether or not the affair was truly finished. In spite of his assertion, I guessed it would not require much of a spark to rekindle it.

'I'm bound to see her sometimes,' he conceded. 'She'll be passing the site quite regularly on her way to work or going home, or I might come across her in town or at Aidensfield ... but we both know the score. We'll keep our distance, Nick.'

'Let's hope you can live up to that promise,' I smiled, adding, 'I haven't seen Deirdre since that night.'

'I think she took the next night off work, claiming a headache or something.'

'I was in the Hopbind a couple of days

ago, but it was at lunchtime and she wasn't behind the bar.'

'I think she'll be keeping out of your way, Nick!' and he smiled, the first smile during that conversation. 'She really is embarrassed by what happened.'

'I don't make a habit of being a Peeping Tom,' I had to say.

'I know. You were doing your job, I appreciate that. So let's forget it, shall we?'

I told him about the latest crane theft and he assured me his were as secure as he could make them. I was pleased I was able to have such an adult and level-headed conversation with Ken. It elevated him in my estimation, but I reckoned it would not be quite so easy coping with Deirdre when we met.

Although I was within a short distance of Gordon and Deirdre's home, I decided not to call but because I was in the dale, I would drive higher into the wilderness to see how Claude Jeremiah's caravan site was progressing. It was some time since I had ventured this way; Ken's reference to the Greengrass caravan project had reminded me about it and I knew that Sergeant Blaketon would quiz me sooner or later about any scheme currently being perpetrated by Greengrass. It was sensible to keep myself fully informed.

When I arrived, two things were immed-iately visible: one was an old and battered cream-coloured caravan with a black metal chimney stack, and the other was a colossal pile of fresh earth. There were tons of the stuff. It was covering the area where I had expected to find a well-prepared concrete or tarmac surface.

It was so large that lorry marks extended to the top and it was clear that the vehicles reversed up the heap to deposit yet more from the summit. It was a growing mountain of fresh earth. I thought Claude was preparing that patch of ground as a base for static caravans. If he was intending to fashion a commercial site, he'd need a toilet block or standpipes at each pitch, and perhaps an office or small shop, but there was no room for anything here. And I wondered whether this monstrous pile had smothered Claude's patch of famous rare flowers.

Anxious to find an answer, I parked my motor bike and walked into the caravan site, the gate standing wide open. I could see lots of lorry tracks leading into it, an indication of the means of arrival of the mountain, and I could trace the lorries' turning circle and their trip to the summit to tip yet more earth upon this growing pile. But the place was deserted. I wandered around the mountain of earth, looked across to the patch of rare flowers which had not been impaired, then peered into the caravan, wiping a window clear of muck to do so. But there was no sign of the proprietor of this esteemed establishment.

As I mounted my motor bike to return to Aidensfield, however, I noticed the familiar shape of Greengrass's truck heading towards me from the reservoir site. It was piled high with fresh earth and so I decided to hang around to see what transpired. Greengrass was at the wheel with Alfred at his side, his flea-ridden dog sitting on the passenger seat and peering through the windscreen. I waited on the rough track outside Claude's piece of ground and when he saw me, I could see the change of expression on his face.

He muttered something to Alfred, something which was probably both obscene and uncomplimentary, but as I could neither lip-read nor hear his words, I chose not to think about it. Once through the gate, he ignored me, pulled into a parking bay, reversed out in the opposite direction and chugged backwards up the slope of the earth mountain. The gradient was shallow enough for his old vehicle to reach the top where Claude operated the tipping mechanism and released his current load of soil. As it slithered to rest down the rear slope, he returned to ground level and halted near me, lowering his window to talk.

'If it's me you want,' he said, 'I've down nowt wrong. This truck's quite legal. I'm not breaking any laws by shifting this topsoil, besides we're not on a public road so the usual rules don't apply!'

'I was just passing, Claude ...'

'Just passing? Hah!' he exclaimed. 'You can't *just* pass this place, you've got to make an effort to get here. So what is it this time? Somebody complaining about mud on the highway or noise or summat else?'

'No complaints, Claude. No trouble. No law breaking. Not even a query about overloading. It's just a social visit, to see how you're getting on. I was interested in the caravan site you were preparing. Remember, you told me about it months ago? I'm interested because tourists often ask me to recommend suitable places where they can stay.'

'Oh, I see, well, that's different. I mean, if we're talking business ...' and he descended from the wagon to join me. Alfred came too but slunk away towards the caravan, hoping to find a bowl of water.

'That was the idea, Claude. But I see you've not made much progress.' I glanced at the huge heap of topsoil to show my concern. 'I see there's no room for more caravans.'

'Aye, well,' and he blinked rapidly for a few moments. 'Yon soil's not a permanent fixture. It's just a temporary storage place until I get it shifted.'

'And your caravan? Ken Rigby says he's going to use that.'

'Aye, he wants to rent it for a few weeks. I said he could shift it from here if he wants to. He can park it on the reservoir site, somewhere close to toilets and fresh tap water and that canteen of his.'

'That'll make more room for your soil project,' I grinned. 'You could start another pile over there, or extend this one!'

'I don't want to start any more piles!' he snapped. 'I want rid of the stuff. That was the idea. To get rid of it.'

'Oh, I thought you were collecting it!'

'Look, it's nowt to do with you why I'm storing tons of topsoil in my land.'

'So long as you've not pinched it,' I couldn't resist that comment.

'Trust you to lower the tone of this conversation! You can ask at the site office: I've got permission to move it.'

'I believe you,' I smiled.

'Look, if you must know, I buy it by the lorryload and my contract says I can sell it. That's how I make money—I buy cheap and sell fast. The profit's mine—these contractors want shot of the stuff anyway and there's enough in that valley to cover half the new gardens in Yorkshire. I'm doing a service by getting rid of my share, even if it's nobbut a drop in the ocean compared with all the stuff they're having to shift.'

'So it's a new business, is it? Selling topsoil?'

'Do you know anybody who might want to buy some?' was his next question.

'Not off-hand,' I said. 'But I'll keep my ears open, I'll refer them to you. How much can you spare?'

'All this lot!' he snapped.

'All of it? But you've enough to cover a whole building site. You could cover hundreds of house gardens, or a football pitch or cricket field ...'

'Aye, well,' and he blinked anew. 'That was the idea. It was this chap I met at Ashfordly mart ...'

'The mart?'

'Well, the pub really, on market day. He was a builder, he's developing a big site on the coast near Strensford, a hundred and fifty new houses, detached and semi-detached, with garages and gardens. He said he wanted some good topsoil because the land on them cliffs is a bit thin ... you know how it is.'

'And you said you could fix him up with

some very good topsoil?'

'Aye, well, that's right enough. It is good stuff. Untilled for centuries, full of natural goodness.'

'So what went wrong?' I had to ask.

'He went broke before he even made a start,' muttered Claude. 'Not one spadeful of ground did he dig before he went bust; summat to do with a development near Bradford.'

'And you're left with tons of topsoil that you can't get rid of?'

'Well, not that I've tried all that hard, not just yet. I've got to shift it from the reservoir basin as fast as I can because if it's left behind, it'll cause a hold-up and I'll be into the penalty clauses. The contractors are shifting their allocation—I've my own allocation which I have to get moved by month end.'

'Think of the profit!' I laughed.

'What profit?' he grunted. 'It's doing nowt but cost me money right now, and instead of delaying yon reservoir, it's delaying my caravan project. I can't start my caravan site until I get all that muck shifted.'

'And you can't shift the mountain of muck because you've not found a buyer?'

'Right,' he said. 'Now, if you don't mind, I've got a lot of muck to shift ...'

'You could always dig a hole and bury it!' I laughed.

'Give over!' he groaned.

'All right. If I hear of anyone who wants a few loads of topsoil, I'll tell them to contact you,' I said, and I meant it.

'I'd appreciate that, Constable, I really would,' he said; and so I bade him farewell.

It was about a week later when I received a call from Sergeant Blaketon.

I had completed a morning's patrol of my Aidensfield patch and was at home for lunch; as I was enjoying my coffee afterwards, the telephone rang. Mary answered it and advised me that Sergeant Blaketon wanted to speak to me. It seems someone had reported a crime on my beat and my attention was required. I went into the office and picked up the telephone.

'PC Rhea, Aidensfield,' I announced myself.

'Sergeant Blaketon, Ashfordly,' came the familiar voice. 'Rhea, get your skates on, you've got a crime to deal with.'

'Right, Sergeant. What's happened?'

'Somebody's nicking fresh topsoil,' he said.

'Not Greengrass?' I asked.

'It's Greengrass it's being nicked from!' he chuckled. 'Now what I should be asking is where or why Greengrass has obtained such a thing. It's not exactly the sort of thing he'd leave lying around that ranch of his.'

'Oh, I know how he's acquired it.' I then explained to my sergeant how Claude had managed to acquire a sizeable hummock of earth, what he had intended to do with it and how he was now unable to get rid of it.

'Then I'd have thought he'd be pleased if somebody was relieving him of the stuff!' laughed Blaketon. 'Anyway, we've had a report of a crime so we must respond, even if the victim is Greengrass.'

'Is it a crime?' I asked him.

'Is what a crime?' He was puzzled by my question.

'Stealing earth,' I replied. 'I thought that things attached to the realty were not larcenable.'

'If what you say is true, the Greengrass cache of soil has already been detached from the realty, therefore it is larcenable. It belongs to him, it's been removed by him and so it can be the subject of larceny, Rhea. So if somebody is helping themselves unlawfully to his gold mine, then we must take the necessary action.'

'Right, Sergeant, I'm on my way. Where is Claude, by the way?'

'He rang me from his home, he'd been

trying to contact you but there was no reply.'

'I was out and Mary was shopping this morning,' I said.

'Well, he said he was going to his caravan site and would wait until a police officer arrived. So over to you, Rhea.'

Claude was not in the best of moods when I hove to upon my little Francis Barnett. I dismounted and walked across to him as he waited beside his truck, taking my notebook from my pocket as I approached him.

'What took you so long?' he snapped. 'I rang Blaketon ages ago.'

'I was out on another job, Claude. I got here just as quickly as I could.'

'Well, why didn't he come? Is a crime of this kind beneath the skills of a sergeant? Or is it because I'm the victim that he's not taking it too seriously? There's no hope of catching 'em now is there? I mean, whoever nicked my soil will be miles away. I thought the idea was to catch 'em red-handed ...'

'So when did it go missing?' I asked.

'How do I know?' he blustered. 'I wasn't here, was I?'

'So when did you miss it?' I tried again. 'When did you last see it here, and when did you notice it had gone?'

'It was here when I packed up the night

before last, half-four or thereabouts, just as it was getting dark. I was away yesterday, on business, and came here at half-eight this morning. That's when I saw it had gone.'

'Enough time for a lorryload of soil to be driven down to London, put on a ferry and used to build a dam in Switzerland or grow tulips in Amsterdam. I doubt if we'd have had much success if we'd chased an invisible load of muck, do you?' I said somewhat facetiously. 'So how much has been stolen?'

'How do I know?' he asked. 'They took a big chunk out of the side of that mound. They must have had a digger to dig it out and load it, and a truck of some kind to carry it away. How much has gone? A lorryload, I'd say.'

'How much is there in a lorryload?' I pressed him. 'A ton? Two tons? More?'

'I never weigh my loads, besides I have no idea how big the lorry was that took it.'

'You should weigh your loads, you might get prosecuted for overloading!'

'Give over! Anyroad, this is private land, the rules of the road don't apply.'

'Just be careful, Claude. Now, the hole that was left? Can we put an amount on that?'

'Two tons,' he snapped. 'Say two tons.'

'And the value?' I asked. 'I need this for my crime report.'

'Value? How can I tell you how much it's worth if I don't know how much has gone?'

'I need an estimate of its value, Claude. One lorryload of topsoil. Two tons. How much would you charge for that?'

'Thirty quid?' He raised his eyebrows and perhaps I could hear his brain ticking over with insurance claims in mind.

'If you say thirty quid, then that's good enough for me,' I said, jotting down the figure in my notebook. 'Now,' I continued with a twinkle in my eye. 'Can you describe it?'

'Describe it?' he burst. 'You can see it for yourself! Or what's been left. It was just like that. A sort of soily-looking colour and texture, with a few dandelion roots in it ... you describe it!'

'Shall I say one lorryload comprising two tons of high grade topsoil, untreated?'

'*Very* high grade topsoil,' he grinned.

'Right, and you'd recognize it if you saw it again?'

'Recognize it? How can I recognize a load of topsoil as mine?'

'Well, if we trace the soil, we have to be sure it is yours before it can be restored to you. And we'd need you to state, beyond any doubt, that it was your soil that we recovered, and that no one had permission to remove it. That's if we are to prosecute the thief.'

'This is getting dafter by the minute!' he growled. 'All I wanted you fellers to do was to get on your bikes and establish a road block or summat, to stop the thieves before they got rid of it.'

'So have you any idea who's taken it?' I asked.

'No, how could I?'

'So you've not seen anyone snooping around your place, asking about topsoil or riding up these lanes on lorries or diggers?'

'No I have not, apart from the construction workers.'

'Right, well, I'll ask around. Someone might have heard something or seen something in your absence.'

'You'll be asking that artist chap and his missus?'

'I will,' I assured him.

'And them fellers on the site?'

'I will indeed.'

'But you'll not set up road blocks and search building sites or visit folks building their rockeries from stuff they nick from the moors ...'

'If we suspect anyone in particular, then we shall visit them and ask where they got their soil, but we can't just rush off into the countryside without a little more information to work on. Now, you'll have to make sure you secure your premises tonight, Claude, otherwise they might be back for more!'

'I've got a padlock for my gate, a brand new 'un,' he said. 'It'll be locked from now on.'

'Good. Well, I'll commence enquiries and in the meantime, I suggest you contact your insurance company; the fact you have reported it to us means they will look with sympathy upon your claim.'

'So you're not going to set up road blocks?'

'Tell me where you suggest we start, and I'll have words with Sergeant Blaketon,' I suggested. 'Or is it better that we make discreet enquiries first?'

'I don't know why I pay my rates for this kind of service. And what about you guarding my property tonight, then? Keeping watch on my soil to see if they come back?'

'That's your responsibility, Claude. You keep watch, and ring me if they turn up.'

'There's no phone up here!'

'I rather suspect the thieves will know that,' I said. 'But I cannot spend all my time sitting and waiting for topsoil thieves, but we will circulate details and we will maintain a close watch on all local roads during the night in the hope that we come across the thieves. Every patrolling officer in this area will be told about these thefts and we do hope we catch them red-handed. You know there's an ongoing epidemic of mobile crane thefts too?'

'Are you telling me they're using 'em to nick my soil?'

'No, not in so many words, but something pretty big is needed to lift your soil from that pile. I'd keep my eyes open if I were you, Claude, you might just drop across a mobile crane doing something unlawful.'

'With my soil?'

'With your soil, Claude,' I said with tongue in cheek.

'Aye, well, if the nation's constabularies are on the lookout, there's just a chance I might get it back!'

I knew, in my heart of hearts, that there was very little chance we would ever find this particular load of topsoil; even if we did, it would be practically impossible to prove it had come from Claude's pile and so we were left with the hope we would catch the thieves as they attempted to dispose of it, or if they returned to bear away more of it under cover of darkness. In spite of those reservations, I had to make an effort to detect the crime and one of the methods was to make enquiries in the vicinity. There was only one dwelling in Ramsdale—the home of Gordon and Deirdre Precious—which meant that my local house-to-house enquiries would not take very long.

When I arrived, Gordon was out on the moors, completing a landscape for a client and Deirdre, with a flush of embarrassment on her cheeks, admitted me to her kitchen. She made a good pretence of making me welcome, offering me a coffee which I accepted, and no doubt pondering, in the initial moments, the reason for my call. As we awaited the boiling of the kettle, I explained.

'Oh,' was her first response. 'Oh, I see. I thought it might be about the other night.'

'How you spend your leisure moments is no concern of mine,' I explained. 'I was sorry to intrude as I did, but I do have to check all suspicious vehicles.'

I told her I'd already spoken to Ken Rigby and that I knew of their plans to stay away from each other. There was the beginning of a tear in her eyes as we talked and she sniffed several times, saying how foolish she had been and how she really did love her husband and she'd never cheat him again. I assured her, as

I had assured Ken, that I would not reveal her indiscretion to Gordon nor indeed to anyone else, and this offered some relief.

'You must think I am terrible, Nick,' she sniffed, as we sat at her kitchen table.

'My job teaches me a lot about human nature,' I heard myself say. 'I would never condemn you, nor would I condemn Ken, but when I saw you together, I must admit my first thought was for Gordon.'

'I know,' she said quietly. 'But it's all over now, we can resume our lives ... thanks for being so understanding.'

I then quizzed her about Claude's missing loads of topsoil, asking if she'd heard any unusual noises in the dale during the night, or seen any suspicious vehicles or people travelling to and from Claude's caravan site. She had not. She explained that she and Gordon occupied the main bedroom at the front, overlooking what would become the new reservoir, and the thickness of the stone walls meant they heard very little; vehicles could pass along the lane behind their home without them ever realizing.

She said she was speaking for Gordon too; if he had heard or seen anything odd, he would have mentioned it to her, but he'd said nothing about any odd goings-on in the dale.

But, she promised, she would bear Claude's loss in mind and if the thieves returned, she would write down a description of them, along with details of their vehicles, including registration numbers. I mentioned the mobile cranes too, not that one would venture along her narrow lane but in her travels, she might encounter one being surreptitiously removed from the reservoir site. I left her after thanking her for her help.

I must admit I was pleased I had reestablished contact with Deirdre and that any lingering embarrassment had now evaporated. Any future meetings would be easier. I was pleased that she and Ken had made such an adult and sensible decision about their future and when I dropped into the site office to make routine enquiries about Claude's loss of soil, I spoke to Ken. I told him I'd spoken to Deirdre only minutes earlier and he understood what I was saying to him—but he could not help me with any information about Claude's loss. Like Deirdre, he said he would keep his eyes open for future villainy.

After leaving Ramsdale, I did make enquiries around the district, particularly at local buildings sites and from people I thought might be in the market for fresh topsoil but I never traced those responsible. Happily, however, no more soil was taken from Claude's pile and I must admit I did sometimes wonder whether he had imagined the loss. A settling of soil, a miniature landslide or even a change of appearance in the shape of the pile due to continuing dumping might have led him into thinking someone had stolen a load, but it was all speculation.

Over the following days, I kept in touch with Claude about my lack of progress, albeit explaining what I had done, and although he grumbled a lot, he did appreciate how difficult it was to recover his topsoil and apprehend those responsible. Having calmed him to that extent, my heart sank when he rang three or four days later.

'Yes, Claude?' I asked. 'How can I help you?'

'There's been another theft from my caravan site!' he snarled.

'How much this time?' I asked.

'Not soil!' he grunted. 'It's that new padlock. They've nicked my new padlock!'

'Do you want me to establish road blocks around the county?' I asked.

'Don't be daft!' he grunted.

'Right, then, can you describe it?' I asked, reaching for my notebook.

8

We only part to meet again.
John Gay (1685–1732)

It was no surprise that Ken Rigby's tenure of Claude Jeremiah's caravan was of exceedingly short duration. Claude's caravan, which was rather like a decaying plywood henhouse on wheels, but not as comfortable, could never be described as desirable accommodation. One of its many defects was Claude's ever-increasing mountain of topsoil. Apart from obscuring views from the windows, the soil had spread across the entrance to the parking area to frustrate any attempt to move the caravan. Without shifting several tons of soggy earth, therefore, it was impossible for Ken to tow his temporary home to a more congenial place.

He tolerated the solitude, discomfort, inconvenience and ever-increasing pile of muck for little more than a fortnight, then by dint of much telephoning and personal contact, managed to obtain a very pleasant room at the Oak Tree Hotel in Ashfordly.

The cosy, traditional but very comfortable old inn with its oak beams and open fires occupied one side of the market-place and overlooked a small stream to the rear. It catered for Ashfordly imbibers as well as tourists, and the regulars could be guaranteed to stage a local yokel act for the benefit of gullible visitors. For Ken, the chief advantage was that the bar was always full of Ashfordly people, male and female, consequently it was a focus of activity throughout the year. Out of the tourist season, the landlord was pleased to have his rooms in use, therefore Ken's arrival was regarded with considerable favour.

I was sure the convivial atmosphere would be to his taste and must admit I wondered if he would find another romance—some Ashfordly ladies were ripe for picking. During one of my visits to his office, he lamented his cold and lonely nights in Claude's caravan but smiled at his joy at finding the Oak Tree. He did tell me, however, that he missed Deirdre while stressing he had been true to his promise not to contact her.

In his days as a guest of Claude Jeremiah Greengrass, Ken had to drive past her house on his way to work but assured me Deirdre had no idea he'd spent two miserable weeks in such close proximity, adding she did not know he was now boarding at the Oak Tree in Ashfordly. She worked in Ashfordly, as I knew, but I was aware that when Sandra North Fashions was open for business, Ken would be working six miles away in the middle of the moors. I also knew that he'd leave the inn each morning to drive to Ramsdale long before Deirdre arrived in Ashfordly and he'd return in the evenings long after she had gone home. The chances of them meeting either in the town or during their journeys to work were therefore remote, so I believed. So far as chance meetings were concerned, I did not envisage the very masculine site foreman wishing to enter Sandra North Fashions in Ashfordly because it was very much a ladies-only emporium. It was full of expensive lingerie, skirts, stockings and the things that only a woman would buy, although some men might venture within to buy their loved one something frothy and flimsy.

But it is always wrong to say categorically something will never happen.

My experience told me that if it was remotely possible for Ken and Deirdre to meet again, however accidentally that might be, then it would happen. In an area with such a low population, it was inevitable. In spite of that, if and when such a meeting did occur, it could be argued the respective parties were not really trying to avoid one another. It might even be said they were doing their best to engineer such a reunion, albeit with all the guile necessary to suggest its casual innocence.

If they did meet again, would it be due to unbridled adult lust or the innocence of true love? I cannot comment because I have no idea of the torment experienced by them in the months they were apart. From time to time, though, whilst remaining mindful of Gordon's role in this affair, I was acutely aware that my action had led to their separation. But was I also responsible for them being reunited—with all the consequences that followed?

Their reunion happened many months after my fateful discovery in the car. As I hadn't seen Ken and Deirdre together since that time, I assumed their romance was over. I was quite sure Deirdre had decided to remain with Gordon in the role she had created for herself but in spite of their reassurances, perhaps I was wrong?

During those months, of course, the dam and reservoir work was proceeding apace. One could see the beginnings of the huge concrete base of the dam deep below ground level and while all this activity continued to shatter the tranquillity of

Ramsdale, I maintained my occasional visits to Gordon. His earnings were increasing and his name was becoming known across a wider area.

He had shown a commendable commercial streak in producing small reproductions of his work, such as postcards and table place settings, and thus he was beginning to enjoy the success for which he strove. Over that winter, spring, summer and autumn I regularly dropped in for coffee and a chat; I had bought several watercolours for myself and my family, some in miniature form, and although we could not be described as close, I do think Gordon valued me as a friend. And throughout, I never hinted that Deirdre had been unfaithful and neither did he. Sometimes, she was in the house when I called and, so far as I could see, the relationship between her and Gordon was happy and calm.

For me, it meant the threat of a domestic drama had subsided. Deirdre was supporting Gordon and he was becoming a success; Ken was overseeing the most remarkable transformation Ramsdale had ever witnessed and the harmonious relationship between the contractors and local people had been maintained. From a professional point of view, I had no complaints. Everything seemed fine, even if the natural features of that lovely dale were changing slowly.

As that mild winter faded from our memories and spring arrived with colour and light, there was a flavour of anticipation in the air. I was sensitive to this and could see that people were beginning to appreciate the new but different beauty of Ramsdale with its man-made lake. Whereas few had visited Ramsdale in the past, many were now contemplating its forthcoming charms. As anticipated, commercial firms were showing an interest in developing lakeside enterprises in conjunction with Swanland Corporation so that future tourists and visitors could be accommodated.

There were rumours of a small marina, for example, with a café and water-ski centre, but Claude had not made any progress with his caravan site. Weeds were now thriving upon the slopes of Mount Greengrass and his solitary caravan remained the only sign of his presence.

During the Easter weekend of that year, I was withdrawn from Aidensfield on the Saturday and instructed by Sergeant Blaketon to patrol Ashfordly on foot. My hours would be 10 a.m. until 6 p.m. with three-quarters of an hour for refreshments, taken at Ashfordly Police Station. I would take sandwiches and a Thermos flask. There was nothing unusual in this—Ashfordly was a mecca for tourists so a police presence was required throughout the twenty-four hours of every public holiday.

I did not mind this duty—time passed quickly because of the interchanges between myself and visitors, particularly those who wanted to know things like the history of the castle, the reason for the monument in the market square and where I kept my truncheon. An added bonus was the Saturday evening off duty, a rare event.

Coincidentally, Deirdre Precious was working in Sandra North Fashions that Easter Saturday, the first really busy day since the Christmas period and her hours were from 9.30 a.m. until 5.30 p.m. She was one of three female staff in the shop—under normal circumstances, I would never have known this tiny facet of Ashfordly's trading life. Later, when reviewing the situation, it did seem the fates were working against poor Gordon. He was spending the day at home with his beloved easel, well away from the crowds.

Ken Digby was also working. Work did not stop at the reservoir over the bank holiday, the only breaks being on Christmas Day and Boxing Day.

That Easter Saturday, therefore, he had expected to be fully engaged on the site but someone from Ken's head office had other ideas. One of the company directors had expressed a wish for a personal meeting with Ken in Ashfordly that day, mixing business with pleasure. He had suggested lunch and so Ken had booked a table for two at the inn where he lodged. The appointment confirmed, Ken therefore made a point of returning to the Oak Tree Hotel to get washed and changed; he and his boss would rendezvous in the bar at 12.30 p.m.

Thus Deirdre, Ken and myself were all in Ashfordly at the same time that Easter Saturday.

And so was old Mrs Carruthers from Aidensfield.

Mrs Carruthers, Florrie to those who knew her, was not a native of Aidensfield, however, having arrived some twenty years ago from Middlesbrough. Upon settling here, she had broadcast to the village that she had retired, aged sixty, from her job in a Teesside clothing factory. She had arrived alone and rented a cottage near the railway station but to this date, no one knows anything about a Mr Carruthers, if indeed there had been one. Whether Florrie was a widow or was divorced or had undergone something rather obscure in the realms of marriage, we never knew. She was well into her eighties and managed on her pension, helped by selling home-made buns in the Aidensfield stores. They were very nice, always spicy and full of currants, and we often treated ourselves to half a dozen of her Aidensfield cakes.

The problem with Florrie was her reputation for being light-fingered.

Although I have every reason to believe her reputation was justified, she had never, to my knowledge, appeared before a court or even been charged with any offences of shoplifting or other types of stealing. I learned of her reputation from Joe Steel, owner of the Aidensfield stores, who would watch her while she pottered around his premises. She, on the other hand, would hang around until another customer entered to distract him when her sleight of hand could make a hen's egg or a tin of soup vanish with more skill than the finest magician. Her ability to make nylon stockings vanish from their sales displays was well known too, both in Aidensfield and Ashfordly. She was known to take things from houses as well—some thought her tactics were nothing more than souvenir hunting because during her visits she would take little things from the kitchen—an egg cup, spoon, box of matches, ballpoint pen or thimble, but rarely cash. Usually, the items were too inexpensive for the losers to bother to inform the police and many accepted Florrie for what she was—a light-fingered thief. I knew of several instances where losers simply took back their own belongings from her house, and she never complained either.

From information gleaned over the years, I knew Florrie was a compulsive thief of small portable articles. There is one tale which perfectly illustrates this. She went into a garage to buy a pint of paraffin for her Primus stove, and when she left (after paying for the paraffin), the proprietor noticed that a sparking plug had vanished from the counter. Why a little old woman without a car would want a sparking plug was rather puzzling, especially as the plug was a dud.

This did illustrate her inability to keep her hands off anything that was both small and portable, and it seems she liked things she could easily hide in her coat, shoes, hat, bag or clothing.

Sometimes she would join a bus trip to Scarborough, Redcar, Saltburn, Whitby or even York and Harrogate. In large towns, her reputation did not precede her although most of the other passengers were aware of her doubtful skills. It was impossible to warn all the shopkeepers in those distant towns but from time to time following her visits, there were crime circulars featuring a little, grey-haired old lady in a purple coat who had rushed out of a shop clutching a box of Elastoplast, a tin of sardines, a bottle of tomato ketchup or some other thing. If Florrie was questioned in such cases, she always denied the crime and had, by then, disposed of the evidence. Cafés were a particularly rich hunting ground for her—knives, forks and spoons vanished almost as soon as she approached a table and when self-service became the norm in our shops, she found new skills at sweet displays and could work wonders with a Mars bar or tube of fruit gums. Although she was never caught on such expeditions, the fact that the stuff disappeared from shelves and displays while she had been on the premises was sufficient for us to point the finger of suspicion at Florrie.

Occasionally, I did wonder what would happen if I succeeded in getting her to court. I felt sure the magistrates, in their infinite wisdom, would look upon her with the utmost lenience, particularly due to her age and the fact she had no criminal record.

They would never know she had a house full of stolen goodies while I would suggest locks and chains were put on all ashtrays in the court's corridors.

It follows that when I saw Florrie pottering around Ashfordly that busy Saturday afternoon, I wondered how many chocolate Easter eggs would disappear into her voluminous clothing or how many spoons she would spirit away from local cafés. I did alert one or two shopkeepers but they'd all seen her—apparently, the tradespeople of Ashfordly had created a type of early-warning system to alert one another to the presence of known shoplifters. This applied whether they were a professional team from West Yorkshire or Teesside, or a lone-operating pensioner from Aidensfield. As I patrolled the town, therefore, I came to realize the shopkeepers were well prepared to deal with Florrie.

The snag was that thousands of other people were also in town. Florrie would make good use of them as a cover for her activities and in that, she was an expert. Try as I might, I could not keep her in sight; she made wonderful use of crowded places, back alleys, rear entrances to shops and cafés, toilets, pubs and other places as she dodged and wove through the streets. I did consider a search of her bags and pockets, but without a specific complaint from a shopkeeper, I would be treading on dangerous ground. Besides, a large male police officer searching a little old lady is not good for our public image, in spite of her culpability. I guessed she would shout and scream to make things appear worse than they were; she might even accuse me of indecently assaulting her!

Extremely wary of the restrictions under which I was compelled to operate, all I could do was wait and watch. Perhaps, if I made myself conspicuous around the marketplace, some shopkeeper would call upon my services if Florrie was caught stealing.

It would be around three o'clock when drama came to Ashfordly market-place. All the players were in position and I was sedately patrolling Bridge Street, using the outside edge of the footpath as I had been taught. This was done for visible daytime patrolling while at night we used the inside edge to keep ourselves within the security of the shadows. As I was proceeding about my duties, Deirdre was inside her shop which was busy with visitors and locals alike, all seeking something rather special for Easter Sunday. At the same time, Ken Digby had just emerged from the dining-room of the Oak Tree Hotel to say farewell to his boss. The Oak Tree was at one side of the square market-place, and Sandra North Fashions was almost directly opposite, on the other side of the square. Ken and boss had had a most enjoyable lunch and as Ken's boss climbed into his car which was parked in the market-place, Ken noticed me. He waved; I saw him and responded, interpreting the wave as a message that Ken wanted to talk to me. From his gestures, I understood he would come across when his visitor had driven away.

To await his pleasure, I halted where I happened to be at that moment, i.e. the pavement outside Sandra North Fashions. I must admit I never thought that either Deirdre or Florrie were inside. Eventually, Ken strode quickly through the crowds; he crossed the road and came to a halt directly in front of me.

'Hi, Nick,' he said affably. 'Glad I caught you.'

'I never expected to see you in town,' I greeted him.

'Business lunch,' he said. 'One of our big wigs wanting some detailed information about the dam's foundations. He could have come to the office, but thought I'd appreciate a working lunch!'

'A nice thought. So, what can I do for you?' I asked.

'One of our men is fifty in a couple of weeks' time. He wants to throw a party in the works canteen, with booze. I know we can have functions there, but I was wondering about the legality of having alcohol on the premises, whether we can sell it for example, either to our own people or to guests ...'

I was about to explain the relevant law to him when the door of Sandra North Fashions burst open and a little, grey-haired old woman hurtled out with astonishing speed. Fleet though she was, she possessed all the control of a beginner on roller skates, i.e. she had no control at all. She crashed into me and threw me off balance; instinctively, I stepped aside to lessen the impact, but collided with Ken who in turn staggered and almost disappeared under a bus whose driver seemed to think that waving his fist and hooting his horn was a useful thing to do. Simultaneously, Deirdre Precious galloped into the street shouting, 'Stop that woman ...'

It is not easy to say precisely what happened next, but I did reach out almost instinctively and found myself clutching the collar of Florrie's overcoat. She was brought to a very abrupt halt as Deirdre collided with her shouting, 'She's a shoplifter ... oh, it's you Nick! Thank God ... hold her, she's been nicking nylons!'

'Right, at last!' I breathed, saying, 'Florrie, come here. You're under arrest ... now, get inside the shop this minute! We're going to search you, all of us ...'

As the air turned bright blue with the onslaught of Florrie's highly choice language, I called to Ken, 'I'll see you later, Ken, about that party ...'

But he was standing in the middle of the pavement with his arms around Deirdre and both were laughing with uncontrolled happiness. My immediate reaction was that this meeting was by no means engineered and I could only marvel at their open joy. But the scene did make me wonder if they'd ever stopped seeing one another ... whatever had happened in the past, they were extremely happy now.

'I'll come in.' Deirdre caught my eye and noted my reading of the situation.

'I'll see you later,' said Ken, and I did not know whether he was talking to me or Deirdre.

To cut short a long story, I struggled into the shop with the squirming, cursing old lady at arm's length, picking up a trail of objects she was discarding as we moved into the premises. She was doing her best to get rid of any evidence I might find upon her, but when I asked her to turn out all her pockets, in the presence of Deirdre Precious, we found some nylons and three pairs of expensive ladies' gloves, all stolen from Deirdre's shop.

The objects she had discarded had been stolen from other shops and cafés—sweets, tea spoons, a tin of mustard powder, a box of Oxo cubes, a cigarette lighter and umpteen other small things were found among her haul. I would have little trouble tracing them to shops in Ashfordly.

Having secured the evidence and found a reliable witness against Florrie, I told her she was going to be reported for summons for stealing the items and she burst into tears. I did not arrest her because that would have meant a trip to the police station followed by possible detention in the cells, at least temporarily, but her detention would require the presence of a policewoman. The nearest was on duty several miles away and she might be committed to some important job at her own station. The detention of any female was always problematical, hence my action to limit the difficulties.

But I had caught Florrie, and that pleased me. Over the years, she had deprived a lot of people of their belongings and deserved a prison sentence, but I knew that would never happen. At a hearing before Eltering Magistrates Court a week later, Florrie was put on probation, her age and clean record being taken into account. When the case was over, she returned to Aidensfield and immediately stole a tube of toothpaste and a bar of soap from Joe Steel's shop. It is true that he never saw her take them—but they were on display when she went into his shop and they'd gone when she left. No one else had been in the shop.

The Florries of this world are unstoppable, they cannot prevent themselves stealing and some fail to see anything wrong in what they do. They seem to think that taking goods from shops is not sinful and not a crime, so how can society teach them otherwise? Locking them up or fining them does not stop them.

After dealing with that minor drama I had time to wonder about the outcome of the collision between Deirdre and Ken.

At the time, I couldn't talk to either at length, although I did visit Ken as I'd promised to sort out the legalities of selling alcohol at a private birthday party in his works canteen. I suggested the party organizer approached a local public house landlord and ask him to apply to the magistrates for an occasional licence. This would allow the licensee to sell alcohol in the works canteen, and the fact that a licensee or a member of staff was in charge would add some kind of control to the event.

While discussing these matters with Ken, he never mentioned Deirdre. I felt he might have made some reference, however short and humorous, about the incident in the street but he didn't. In retrospect, that was rather suspicious—our conversation that day was not rushed or interrupted and he had ample time to mention Deirdre if he'd wanted to, if only to ask if I'd seen her or talked to her recently. My interpretation of his silence was that he wanted to resume his friendship with her—or that he had already done so.

Over the next few months, I did see Ken in his site office and Deirdre either behind the bar of the Hopbind Inn or in Ashfordly as she took a break from her shop work. I chatted to each very frequently, the humorous incident with Florrie having apparently wiped away the embarrassment of my discovery of them in the car. But from that moment, I never saw them together. In some ways, I considered that rather strange because, if their reaction outside Sandra North Fashions was an indicator, they were still deeply in love. But, I reasoned, if they were never seen together, was it because they were now being extremely careful?

Perhaps they never met in this area? Perhaps their liaisons were a long way from home? As I pondered this, I realized I had never seen Ken in the Hopbind while Deirdre was working behind the bar. I had never seen them chatting in town or having a snatched conversation in Aidensfield or Ramsdale. I had never seen them together at any of the race-meetings and, so far as I knew, they never joined the same outings or attended the same parties. If they were continuing their relationship, then it was being conducted very secretively. But was the affair continuing? I had no idea and it was not the sort of question I could ask in the village. If I wanted an answer, I'd have to maintain very discreet observations.

Over the months, I continued to drop in for chats and coffee with Gordon Precious who seemed totally content with his new life, and not once did he suggest problems between himself and Deirdre, or that Deirdre was being unfaithful. He spoke about her with his usual love and admiration, praising her for her support and for the long hours she worked so that he could further his career. I was sure Gordon had no knowledge of Deirdre's earlier diversion but, as he chatted, I realized there were thousands of occasions when Deirdre could play away from home. He referred to her working overtime, she would often go away with friends, shopping in Harrogate or York, or even to London to visit the theatre. Most certainly, she was not tied to Gordon or the house and, similarly, he was frequently away. He went to exhibitions or gave lectures about his work; he had been recruited as a tutor for some art evening classes in Ashfordly and, of course, he did venture on to the moors and into the dales to work on his watercolours, sometimes spending an entire day away from home.

If either had wanted an affair, there were ample opportunities.

As I kept the likelihood at the back of my mind, the Greengrass project continued to intrigue me because, after increasing its girth apparently without end over the months, his pile of muck began to dwindle. Upon making enquiries, I discovered he had found someone to purchase his topsoil and over the weeks, Claude's mountain of muck began to shrink lorryload by lorryload. I learned it was to form the basis of a new nursery and garden centre near Eltering, and this made Claude much happier. He did spend some nights in his caravan so he could go early-morning rabbiting and he also spent time collecting and selling items of scrap abandoned upon the reservoir site by the contractors. It was amazing, the stuff that was found while clearing the floor of the dale—apart from the contractors' litter, several old mangles were unearthed, along with oil drums, car wheels and cart wheels, bits of tractors and parts of ploughs, stone troughs, hemmels and large pieces of corrugated iron roofing, the latter probably having taken flight in a gale long ago. Being Claude, he kept most of it in the hope he could sell it to dealers or collectors. In that way, he helped keep the site tidier than it might have been, although with regard to his own business empire, there was still no sign of the hardstandings which were necessary if he was to develop a caravan park. I wondered if there were planning problems but that formed no part of my police duties.

In the ensuing months, the emergent structure in the dale began to look like a dam. After the course of the beck had been diverted and the foundations completed, work began on the huge base.

Massive granite rocks were imported, the kind which formed piers and sea defences at places like Whitby and Scarborough but colossal concrete slabs were also utilized. As time went by, I could discern the distinctive shape of a dam. With a broad base, a rock-filled interior, sluices for the water and other internal necessities, it was, in essence, a huge, solid and well-built wall constructed with a slight curve which faced upstream. It was designed to withstand the pressure of millions of gallons of water which would rise behind it and it was the task of the builders to ensure the dam was impregnable and strong enough to withstand the mighty forces which would be permanently pitted against it. The front of the dam would comprise colossal stones which would eventually blend with its moorland surroundings. Huge oblong rocks of granite would be utilized, making the dam appear, from a distance, to match the dry-stone walls which dominated the surrounding moors. At one end, on the right when facing the dam from downstream, there would be a space large enough to accommodate the coffin of Warwick Humbert Ravenswood, while matching it at the other end would be a stone of like size which would eventually bear a commemorative inscription. The inscription on Warwick's final resting place would match it.

Below the dam, built on to an extension of the main structure, would be huge platforms upon which would be the powerhouse, transformers and offices. At one end of the dam, the end reaching the slopes opposite Ramsdale House, there would be the spillway, a means of preventing an overflow should a surplus of water ever arise.

I found the work very fascinating, particularly the design of pools called stilling basins—these were below the dam and their purpose was to accommodate any overflow in such a way that the velocity and force of incoming water did not cause dangerous erosion to the bed of the stream. Even as the dam was rising from the moorland, the upstream portion—the vast basin which would contain the reservoir—had been virtually cleared of vegetation, earth, trees, stone walls and all the other accoutrements of a former cultivated Yorkshire dale.

Continuing geological tests had been made to ensure the basin would be strong enough to contain the enormous weight of water which would collect—this area was rich with limestone and there were many underground caverns, some empty and others full of water, but no such cavern existed below Ramsdale. Every test showed the dale could cope with the immense weight soon to be imposed upon it, while the sides of the dale, soon to become sides of a huge natural basin, were also solidly waterproof. There would be no discernible leakage from this reservoir.

While all this work and change was happening, Gordon Precious continued to visit the site to depict the major changes and I undertook my routine police duties. Time passed; I worked days, nights, weekends and bank holidays; I dealt with road accidents, motoring offences, sudden deaths, petty crimes, petty vandalism, liquor licensing offences and supervision, some housebreakings, shopbreakings and even a rape. I visited farmers to check their livestock registers, firearms and pig licences. I attended court and race-meetings, I undertook special duties at the seaside, at festivals, agricultural shows and other public gatherings.

Between times I patrolled my patch both on foot, on my Francis Barnet motor bike and later in a mini-van. People died, were married and were born. and before I realized it, four years had passed since the beginning of construction of the Ramsdale Reservoir. At the end of that period, the dam had assumed a handsome, sturdy but surprisingly graceful curved appearance. The stream had been rerouted to its original course and the reservoir was being filled, albeit slowly. The process of filling the reservoir was done in stages with hundreds of tests being conducted as the water rose behind the huge new wall of concrete and granite. And as it rose behind the dam, it spread across the basin which had been prepared for it.

It meant Ramsdale now had a lake, albeit a shallow one, but it was a lake which was expanding slowly as every day went by. For the contractors, it was a tense time; if there were problems with leakages either through the ground or in the man-made features, or problems with the structure of the dam itself, this was when they would be revealed. I visited Ramsdale from time to time, noting that upon each occasion the level of the lake was slightly higher than previously and that the water had spread further towards its eventual limits. Even at this early stage, waterfowl like mallard and moorhens had made their homes beside the reservoir and flocks of black headed gulls were regular visitors. Slightly rippled by the ever-present moorland breeze, the surface of the lake became a beautiful blue beneath the clear skies and I must admit I was proud of the reservoir. On the occasions I popped in to see Gordon, I found him painting the changing scene, recording it for posterity in all its moods, often with the schoolgirl cyclists in the picture.

Having not seen Deirdre with Ken Rigby over those months, I must admit I had forgotten about their early affair; similarly, the reception they gave one another in Ashfordly had also faded in my memory. Deirdre seemed to be working happily at her various jobs and Gordon's work was selling well in the local towns; he had an annual exhibition and was in demand as a speaker and lecturer.

Life, for them both, seemed perfect.

Then, unexpectedly, I found myself

nominated for a refresher driving course. It was for three full days and it would involve three constables plus one advanced driving instructor from our Road Traffic Division. We would use one of the Force's fleet of Ford Zephyrs. Each morning around 9 a.m. I would be collected from my home by the car and would be returned each night around 5 p.m. During the day, with the instructor in the front passenger seat, we would take turns driving in all conditions, town and country alike, at high speed on the main roads, at low speeds in country lanes and on the skid-pan. We'd be put through regular tests; we had to provide a commentary while we were driving and the overall purpose was to have our multiple faults corrected. It was an enjoyable break from routine which would conclude with an individual half-hour test.

On the middle day, we did what was called the long run. This involved a drive across the Pennines into the Lake District where we had lunch in a lakeland café before returning to the North Riding later in the day. We made full use of main roads, byroads, villages and towns in our testing routine, but it was enjoyable.

The drive through the splendour of the Pennines is always popular, many Yorkshire people regularly making the trip for a day's visit to Keswick, Ambleside,

Windermere, Grasmere and elsewhere.

In our case, lunch was in a café below Aira Force and on the shores of Ullswater. We were allowed to wear civilian jackets while having our meal but as we continued to wear blue shirts, black ties and police trousers, civilian jackets were hardly a disguise. Even so, we felt it made us less conspicuous among the hikers and ramblers—even if there was a big police car in full livery parked outside. The café had tables both indoors and out, but we elected to use an indoor table nicely tucked into a corner but with views towards the lake. We bought soup, sandwiches, cakes and coffee from the counter and adjourned to our table to enjoy the meal.

From my seat, I could see the arrival of cars outside, some of which dropped their passengers before heading to the car-park behind the café. Then I had a shock. I saw Ken Rigby's car arrive with him at the wheel. And in the front passenger seat was Deirdre Precious.

9

When I consider life, 'tis all a cheat;
Yet, fool'd with hope, men favour the
deceit ...

John Dryden (1631–1700)

Ken and Deirdre settled on a table outside where a waitress quickly attended to their order. Whereas my colleagues and I took an official but sedate three-quarters of an hour to savour our meal, Ken and Deirdre completed theirs in little more than twenty minutes. Afterwards, they bought bars of chocolate, apples and canned drinks, then left, unaware of my presence. I saw them hand in hand, heading towards the car-park probably with the intention of visiting the lovely Aira Force. There is a wonderful climb through the woods and the spectacular falls are certainly worth a visit.

Upon completion of that refresher course and having achieved the necessary standards, I pondered my lakeland discovery for some time. One half of me said there was nothing intrinsically wrong in a couple of friends having a pleasant day in the Lake District, even if they were a married woman with a man who was not her husband. Contrariwise, the other half of me said they were doing wrong, even if they were merely walking and talking. However innocently it was disguised, this outing was just another stage in their affair and if it had survived almost from the beginning of the work on the reservoir, Gordon must have nursed some suspicions about his wife. If not, how had Deirdre managed to maintain such an enduring secret?

Her behaviour must have changed although, I suppose, Gordon might think it was due to their move to Ramsdale and the uncertainties of the new life they'd created.

In the following weeks, I didn't see Deirdre in Ken's company but I did see them individually. I came across them occasionally during my daily routine and did visit Gordon from time to time but I never told Deirdre or Ken that I had seen them in the café near Ullswater. It was a mistake for them to be seen by me and it might be described as sheer bad luck on their part, but if they could make one mistake, I told myself, they could make another. I might come across them again, or they could be seen by someone else.

Or they might be discovered by Gordon. Or by someone who knew Gordon. There were many permutations and I felt that few people would keep the secret in the way that I had done.

The crux of the matter was that if Ken and Deirdre persisted in their affair, then the unfortunate Gordon would be hurt. I felt increasingly sorry for him and I wondered if there was anything I could do or should do, and yet repeatedly told myself not to get involved with his domestic life. Even if we had become friendly enough to enjoy informal chats, I was always conscious of my role as a policeman. Impartiality when on duty is important; even when off duty, there are difficulties in dealing with the domestic problems of others and I hoped I would be able to remain impartial when the proverbial balloon went up! And up it would surely go!

Some weeks later, when I called on Gordon to enjoy our usual mug of coffee and a chatter, I realized he was not his normal affable or confident self.

He wasn't painting, for one thing. That was a departure from his routine—on every other occasion I'd called, he'd been working. That day, therefore, he admitted me to his kitchen and made a couple of coffees, but as he busied himself with the kettle and mugs I sensed something was wrong. I studied him for a while, noting that he was quieter than normal and almost morose. I guessed he was brooding over some very personal matter—perhaps a commission that had failed to materialize or a disaster with one of his works—and then he managed a smile.

'Sorry, Nick,' he said. 'I'm not much company ... forgive me.'

'Something wrong?'

He did not reply for a long time, then asked, 'Is it that obvious?'

'Something's bothering you.' I watched as he settled at the kitchen table opposite me. He handed me my coffee with a weak smile, then said, 'Nick, you're probably the only true friend I've got. I have to talk to somebody. I don't want you to mention this to a soul, especially not to Deirdre, but if you suspected your wife was cheating you—with another man—what would you do?'

'That's a real poser.' With the knowledge I had so long kept to myself, I did not know how to react to his question. 'If we're talking about real people, I don't think my wife would ever do that ...'

'No, I know she wouldn't but, well, I wasn't suggesting that. What I mean is, I want you to treat this as a hypothetical example. So what would you do? Please tell me, it is important.'

'Well, if it was mere suspicion, I think I would need to find out if there was any truth in it. There's nothing worse than unresolved suspicion; it can demolish any person, man or woman. It's like a cancer gnawing at you.'

'Yes, it is ...' he almost whispered.

'And it's made far worse if it's some suspicion which has no genuine foundation. Suspicion based on rumour or speculation is terrible. So, yes, I would start by setting out to discover out whether or not there was any truth in those suspicions.'

'I've done that,' he said quietly.

'What are you saying, Gordon?'

'I'm saying Deirdre is having an affair, Nick, and it's devastating me. I can't work for thinking about it. I just can't concentrate ... I've tried to shake off my suspicions, God knows I've tried, but it's little things. Lies she's been telling me, her normal behaviour's changed, she been buying sexy underwear, spending lots more time making herself up, having more hair-do's, using more perfume, dressing differently, all sorts of little things, Nick, changes in her behaviour ...'

'Are you sure? You've not misread the signs, have you? I'm sure she'd never hurt you, Gordon, she's so proud of you.'

'She is; she often says so ...'

'Maybe you've misunderstood her actions?' At this point, I began to feel guilty because I was also cheating Gordon but my professional caution compelled me to withhold my knowledge. Nonetheless. I did agonize over whether or not I should reveal what I knew of Deirdre and Ken. But Gordon was continuing.

'That's what I've tried to tell myself. I've told myself I'm being silly, that I'm finding cause for suspicion when there is none. I did think it was her reaction to the move out to Ramsdale, it is a bit remote, but the more I delve into things, the more I examine her behaviour, the more sure I am about what's happening, Nick. Looking back over, oh, several months, there are things that don't add up, things she's done and said, places she's said she's been, people she said she's been with, when she hasn't. Things like that do add up, they add up to the fact she's having an affair. I don't know what to do, Nick. I just don't.'

'Have you tackled her about it?' was my next question. He paused for a moment, sipping from his coffee, then shook his head.

'No, how can I? How can I do that? How can I accuse her of cheating me if she's not? I might have misinterpreted the signs ...'

'You could always hire a private detective,' I said. 'But that's expensive.'

'I couldn't do that. I couldn't spy on her, not my own wife.'

He sat before me with his hands wrapped around the mug, not drinking his coffee but staring into space as he spoke. He was behaving very calmly, dry-eyed the whole time and quite rational, but I could see that he was deeply hurt.

'Gordon, you tell me you have grave suspicions about Deirdre, suspicions which have developed over a considerable time, and yet you still doubt your interpretation of those suspicions ...'

'Maybe I don't want to believe them,' he said. 'Maybe I don't want to believe she's deceiving me, maybe I can't accept that she's having an affair with another man. And I can't. I can't bear the thought of it, that someone else is touching her, making love to her ...'

'But you do want to know? You want to know if your suspicions are correct?'

He nodded.

'What sort of things have led you to this conclusion?' I asked.

'It's difficult to be precise; it's been happening over such a long period. She's been working late at the pub, getting lifts home with men, for example. There's whispered phone calls, unexplained incoming phone calls. One day, she told me she was going on a shopping expedition to Harrogate with a couple of friends, women friends, and later one of them told me she'd been in London that weekend. The friend, I mean, not Deirdre. She couldn't have been with Deirdre in Harrogate—so I don't know where Deirdre went that day. I didn't ask. I didn't put her on the spot but it made me think she was keeping secrets. It's things like that, Nick, tiny things strengthened by lies. Lots of lies and few straight answers.'

'And have you any idea who she might be seeing?' I had to ask.

'No, no idea. But she does meet a lot of men in her pub work ... and I would never want her to stop that work, she enjoys it and likes the companionship. She needs something like that, living out here. Besides, the money does give her some independence.'

He stared into space again and I wondered how to tackle this dilemma, but concluded there was only one way for Gordon to make any progress.

'You'll have to ask her,' I told him. 'It's the only way.'

'I couldn't, Nick! I just could not do that.'

'Well, if you don't have her followed by a detective, then you'll have to do it yourself.

You've got to find out whether there are any genuine grounds for your suspicions. When you are reasonably confident she's going to meet her man friend, you follow her, or you test out her story, initially without her knowing. It won't be easy, Gordon, in fact it will be extremely difficult and heart-breaking if you do find your suspicions are correct.'

'You couldn't do it, could you? For me? Keep an eye on her for me? Watch her and let me know if she is seeing somebody?'

'Sorry, Gordon,' I had to say. 'Much as I'd like to help you, Police Regulations forbid me doing that sort of thing.'

'But if you saw Deirdre in circumstances which you knew were suspicious, with a man, I mean, meeting secretly, that sort of thing, you'd tell me?'

I gripped my mug so tightly that my fingers began to turn white but had to shake my head.

'It's a hypothetical question, Gordon, and I'm not sure of the answer. Looking back on my own experiences with this kind of problem—professional experiences, I might add—I don't think I would tell you. If I saw Deirdre in what I thought were adulterous circumstances, my interpretation of the event might be wrong. If I saw her having dinner at a nice restaurant with a man, for example, it might be nothing more than that. It might be a meeting to do with her work, or she might be meeting a relation ... there are hundreds of perfectly acceptable reasons why men and women meet those of the opposite sex who are not their spouses, and it doesn't mean they are having affairs. If I did see her in such circumstances and relayed the information to you, I could be utterly mistaken and so could you—and think of the damage that would cause, think of the distrust it would needlessly generate between you and Deirdre.'

'I take your point. You're right, it is my problem and I've got to sort it out,' he whispered. 'The trouble is I can't distinguish what might be part of an affair and what might not.'

'It's very important you do make that distinction,' I went on. 'It means that, on balance, Gordon, I don't think I would tell you—the reason would be simple as I've just explained. The wrong interpretation could be placed on what I had witnessed and think of the problems that would cause.'

'But I thought the police gave evidence in such cases ...'

'If a police officer witnesses something in the course of his duty which might be relevant to a domestic court case, then he could be called upon to give

238

evidence in court or at a tribunal, just like anyone else.'

'But individuals can't expect the police to spy on their partners?'

'No. Any evidence we would give would have to be part of formal legal proceedings. But a police officer must not keep watch on people for domestic purposes, it's not part of our duty. We could never keep an eye on a man's wife to determine whether or not she was committing adultery, for example. It's up to you to find out if there is any truth in your suspicions. I'm sure you can achieve that without asking Deirdre if she's having an affair. When you feel you have the necessary proof, that's the time to confront her.'

'And ask her to end it?'

'*Tell* her to end it,' I said.

'And if she doesn't?'

'I don't know.' I had to be honest. 'All I do know is that many affairs are short-lived, they are seldom enduring. Many of those involved do return to their spouses and sometimes, a marriage can be stronger because of it. Sometimes.'

'I could never imagine that!' he cried. 'It would devastate me. Look at me now, even before I've reached that stage! I'm a wreck; I can't work; I don't know what to do.'

'You've made an important step by

239

talking about it,' I assured him. 'You mustn't keep such things to yourself, that's guaranteed to aggravate matters.'

'I had to talk to somebody and thank God you turned up when you did. Oh, God, this is awful ... you've no idea of the agony I'm suffering. I just cannot believe what she's doing.'

'Then get proof, Gordon, get the necessary proof before you do anything else. That's vital. And be rational about it, don't do anything silly.'

'Like jumping off a cliff, you mean? No, I won't do that. But I can talk to you about it, can I? Like this? As friends?'

'Yes, of course you can, and I'm sure you can distinguish between what is part of my duty and what is not.'

'I know you'll tell me anyway,' and he smiled wanly.

'Now, you should get your painting gear assembled and go on to the moors to paint a very angry picture.'

'You could be right,' he smiled, taking my empty mug from me. He went across to the sink and placed it in a bowl. 'You'll call again?'

'I will,' I promised, adding, 'And you can call and see me any time, you know that? Or just ring if you'd like to talk.'

'Thanks,' he said, and I knew he was depending on me. That meant I would have to be extremely careful how I handled this delicate matter. I'd have to strive for a balance between my police duties and my genuine concern for Gordon. I left him to his misery knowing there was so little I could do at this stage. Sooner or later he would learn the truth and I wondered how he would react although it was perhaps a good thing that he'd had this opportunity to prepare himself for the worst. That, I felt, was far better than the sudden shock of discovering the truth. I wondered how Gordon would cope with a sudden shock.

In the meantime, Phase III, construction of the dam itself, was nearing completion. This meant it looked like a dam and worked like a dam, even if the water had not yet risen to its full height behind it, and that the service accommodation (Phase IV) was not yet complete. Although water was accumulating, it would be a long time before the reservoir was full. At this stage, the movement of water was being controlled; it passed through the sluices in a regulated flow and the effect, downstream, meant that the appearance of Ramsdale Beck had not radically altered. Below the dam, the flow was very similar to those days, now long ago, when there had been no reservoir in the upper dale.

Long before the reservoir was allowed to fill to capacity, the elegant stone structure, already known as Ramsdale Bridge Dam, had to be thoroughly tested for the effects of gravity, hydrostatic pressure stresses and a force known as uplift in addition to stresses within the ground itself. The sheer weight of the dam and of the accumulated water could produce powerful forces within the ground and while these were being assessed, so was the likelihood of various other strains and leakages. All these had to be checked and double-checked before the level of water was allowed to rise any further.

Under no circumstances must the weight and content of water, or the result of subterranean, hydrostatic or other stresses, be allowed to produce a breach of the dam and no leak, however minor, must be permitted. If any of that happened and the dam burst, then a twenty-foot high wall of water would sweep down the dale with catastrophic results for Aidensfield and district.

As a mere village constable, I had no idea of the precise form or content of those stringent tests, except that they were diligently carried out over a long period by teams of experts. None of the tests was made known to the public, but I did know that it was a lengthy and demanding process which demanded the highest degree of skill from those responsible. I had absolute faith in the construction teams.

I was not sure whether there had been the equivalent of a topping-out ceremony as there is when the roof of a new house is completed but in fact, the dam was far from complete. There was an immense amount to do, including completion of the powerhouse and transformer. Added to that, I could not forget the eventual interment of the mortal remains of Warwick Humbert Ravenswood, currently languishing in a mortuary freezer.

The wide and deep oblong hole which would accommodate his remains could be seen, but only from a great distance. It was virtually invisible from the walkway itself, for it was in the face of the dam immediately below the walkway and beneath one support of the old pack-horse bridge. Some eight feet long by four feet high and four feet deep, it looked like a massive gaping mouth in the neat stonework. It was prominent at this stage because no stone sealed it—that would come after Warwick had been placed inside. Nonetheless, the reconstruction and re-siting of Ramsdale Bridge was now complete. It was located at the eastern end of the dam and when the dam was finished, there would be a walkway across the top. Its route would be beneath the old pack-horse bridge and would be duly fenced for safety purposes, with a small office complex, viewing platform and inspection chambers.

The public could cross the dale via that route which, in effect, had replaced the old track. Someone jokingly suggested it should be called the Ravenswood Walk in honour of the man whose bones would be forever built into the stonework below it—and the joke became reality because that is what the walkway was eventually called. I did think the little bridge added an aura of charm to the new structure, a well executed blending of old and new.

In the weeks following my emotional talk with Gordon, I did make a conscious effort to visit him whenever I was in Ramsdale but he was always away from home. The house was deserted—Deirdre was working either in Sandra North Fashions or at the Hopbind—but I did not regard Gordon's absence as unusual because he did go out quite regularly, either to paint, lecture or run his art classes. His absences did mean, of course, that I was not updated with developments in his marriage, but conversely, he did not telephone me to ask for a chat. This led me to believe he had resolved the matter.

Then one dull and dreary evening in late April, an hour or so after sunset, I received a telephone call from Deirdre. I was on duty, finalizing some paperwork in my office before knocking off at 10 p.m.

'Nick?' she began in a little, squeaky voice. 'I'm worried about Gordon.'

'Why?' was my first reaction. 'What's happened?'

'He went out this morning, on to the moors to do some work, and he's not come back. He always gets back in good time, he can't work in the dark, of course. It's not like him to be so late. I'm worried about him.'

'He's not been missing overnight, then?'

'Oh, no, nothing like that. But if he's going to be late, or thinks he might be, he always leaves a note to say where he's gone. This time, he hasn't. I wouldn't have rung you otherwise.'

'I'll come straight away,' I told her. 'You're at home now?'

'Yes, it was my half day at the shop, I've got the afternoon off and I'm not working at the Hopbind tonight. Thanks. See you soon.'

It was pouring down as I passed the reservoir site, but the place was brightly lit to give it a warm glow in the darkness which had now descended. The site huts and offices were all illuminated and

245

powerful floodlights highlighted the stone beauty of the curved dam with its topping of the old bridge. Some of the lights played on the shallow water behind to provide a strangely tranquil scene. The beauty of the floodlit water was such a contrast to the bleakness of the dark, deserted moorland which surrounded it but I had no time to admire it. I chugged along, now thankfully in a mini-van as the rain lashed down around me, and eventually came to Ramsdale House. Like the reservoir site, it was brightly lit and I parked in the paddock as usual, hurrying through the gate to the door I normally used. I rattled the brass knocker and Deirdre appeared with a glass of gin and tonic in her hands.

'Come in,' she invited with a wan smile, stepping back to admit me. 'Hurry, Nick, you'll get drenched!'

'Any news of Gordon?' I asked, as I stepped over the threshold to shake the rainwater from my jacket.

'Not a whisper,' she shook her head. 'I hope I'm not being a nuisance.'

'Not at all,' I assured her, then asked, 'Are you alone?'

She nodded and produced another of those wan smiles before adding, 'Did you expect Ken to be here?'

'It was the drink,' I said. 'I wondered if you had company.'

'No, I needed something strong. How about you? Wine? I've red or white?'

'I'll have one glass of dry white, thanks, but no more. I'm on duty and I'm driving.'

She led me into the comfortable lounge where a coal fire was burning. Topped with logs, it produced deep shadows which flickered about the room to produce a most welcoming and warming effect. The light dancing from the oak beams above created deep contrasts between the far corners and the clip rug spread before the fireplace. She indicated the settee and I settled upon it while she poured my wine.

'You're probably thinking I'm making too much of a fuss much too early.' She sat on the floor, curling her trousered legs beneath her as she basked in the glow of the fire. 'He's late home from work, that's all.'

'You know him better than anyone else,' I sympathized. 'You'd not call me without good cause. It is a shocking night.'

'I am worried, Nick, truly,' and she paused now, gazing into the flames and fiddling with the glass in her hands. 'He knows, you know, about me and Ken. I think that's behind it.'

'How did he find out?' I asked.

'He became suspicious; that's not surprising is it? He began to check up on me, check my story every time I went out, every time I did something different. And he followed me sometimes.'

'He's known a long time,' I told her. 'He did talk to me about it, he wanted my advice.'

'Did he?' There was a momentary flicker of anger in her eyes as I revealed this.

'I told him nothing, Deirdre,' I added quickly. 'I did not mention the night I found you with Ken. I knew about your affair but I never told Gordon, I know how to keep a secret but I might have been influenced by Ken's assurance that it was all over.'

'It was, for a time. We didn't see one another for ages. I was desperately worried about Gordon so me and Ken decided to end it ... well, we tried, we really did. He moved out, as you know, and I changed my job ... but, well, we couldn't give one another up, Nick. It all started again with a lot more care about where we met. I'm sorry, you shouldn't be dragged into all this.'

'I saw you at Ullswater,' I told her. 'With Ken.'

'You did? How?'

I explained about the driving course and the sheer coincidence of that brief encounter, then said, 'But I didn't tell Gordon about that either,' I assured her.

248

'So far as I was concerned, you were two friends going for a walk. On that occasion, I did not see you in a compromising position so there was nothing to tell him.'

'So if you didn't tell him about me and Ken, what did you tell him?'

Before I answered that, I asked, 'Does he know the other man is Ken? When he talked to me, he had no idea who you were seeing.'

'Yes, he knows.' She hung her head. 'He was shocked, Nick, deeply shocked and terribly upset. Ken was so nice to him when he went to the site to paint.'

I told her about my conversation with Gordon, explaining that I'd advised him to check the truth of his suspicions before taking any further action. I added that a police officer cannot get involved in domestic matters of this kind.

'Thanks,' she said.

'Thanks? Why?' I asked.

'For doing your best to protect me.'

'And Gordon,' I added. 'I was protecting Gordon. I felt he was vulnerable. And I did believe the affair was over, you know, I didn't want to open old wounds.'

'It's all academic now anyway because he knows all about it, and knows it's Ken. But, can you believe this, I do love Gordon and I don't want him to come to any harm.'

'You think he might? Come to some harm, I mean.'

'That's why I called you,' she said quietly. 'He has been very upset lately, extremely upset and unable to work properly or think straight or even to stay in the same house as me ... when I'm here, he goes out. I've really hurt him, Nick. And I'm mortified by it all, really I am, I'm so ashamed of my behaviour ...'

And she burst into tears.

She placed the glass on the hearth where the reflection of the flames danced in the spirit and then she eased a tiny handkerchief from her sleeve. She blew her nose noisily; I was tempted to go across and comfort her, but realized such an action might be misinterpreted. So I sat and waited for her to compose herself.

Eventually I said, 'Under normal circumstances, you wouldn't have worried if he'd been this late home?'

She shook her head and sniffed back her tears.

I continued, 'I need to know the background in case I have to justify a search party,' I told her. 'Sergeant Blaketon would never sanction a large search simply because a grown man was late home. There have to be some extenuating circumstances.'

'I can understand that,' she sobbed. 'I am so worried about him, Nick. He is prone to depression, you see. Sometimes, he suffers from deep, very black moods, especially when he's under pressure.'

'Right, then we'll do something about it,' I said, draining my glass. 'Now, has he taken anything?'

'Like what?' she blinked at me.

'Overnight things, razor, toothbrush, underwear, extra clothes ...?'

'I don't know,' she said. 'Shall we have a look?'

We checked the bathroom and bedroom and discovered he had not made provision for an overnight absence; he had not even taken his painting materials, his sole possessions being the clothes he stood up in.

They comprised a warm sweater, waterproof cagoule and leggings, hiking boots, woolly cap and a knapsack. She added that some food had gone from the pantry mentioning slices of bread, cheese, some buns, apples and a bottle of blackcurrant juice.

'Any idea where he might have gone?' I asked, as we returned to the lounge.

'It could be anywhere,' she said. 'He's not taken the car, I was using that, and we've an old bike, a push bike, but that's still in the shed. So he's on foot.'

'And his paintings? Has he been working on a particular picture, a scene he'd want to check in some way? Was he painting from a particular vantage point he wanted to revisit?'

'Not to my knowledge,' she said, 'although there is an unfinished one on his easel in the studio, a dark, brooding sort of scene with storm clouds. I've no idea where it is supposed to depict.'

'So he could be anywhere?'

'Yes,' she said weakly. 'That's my worry. If I knew where he was, I'd have gone myself.'

'And Ken? Have you told Ken?'

'What about? Gordon knowing about us, or that Gordon's gone missing?'

'Well, both; they do seem to be connected.'

'No, Ken doesn't know. I should tell him, shouldn't I?'

'Under the circumstances, yes. He ought to know. Gordon wouldn't harm Ken, would he?' I asked after that thought had struck me.

She shook her head. 'I'm going to end it this time. Nick, I really am, once and for all. I can't bear what I've done to Gordon. I've been so stupid, so selfish.

It was just a fling, a bit of excitement, sexual excitement, I suppose ...'

'Let's get him found before we start thinking beyond tonight,' I said. 'Now, we need a starting point. I can't search the entire moorland alone, neither can you. You should stay here, near the telephone, in case he rings or returns. We need a point of contact. He could have fallen and broken a leg or something, or simply overlooked the passage of time.'

'Will it get into the papers?' she suddenly asked.

'The hunt might, but the reason for his disappearance need not,' I said. 'No one apart from you, me, my sergeant and Gordon need know the background to this.'

'Good. I deserve to be criticized, but I must think of Gordon. Yes, so I'll stay here. What will you do?'

'I'll ring Sergeant Blaketon from here, if I may, to tell him what's happened and to ask if he will authorize me to call out the Moors Search and Rescue Team. It takes time for them to assemble, and then we'll need some kind of plan based on where Gordon was last seen or known to have gone.'

And so began the hunt for Gordon Precious.

Gordon was found at one o'clock the following morning lying in a gully on the moors above Gelderslack. He was alive but was found to be suffering from a badly bruised head, a broken right leg and hypothermia.

It seemed that, in the misty rain-filled darkness, he had fallen into the gully to suffer the broken bone and other injuries, and he had been unable to crawl out to raise the alarm. He'd lain there for most of the day and night in cold, foggy and wet conditions, this producing hypothermia in spite of his clothing and good health. He was taken to Strensford Cottage Hospital for treatment and I had the pleasant task of telling Deirdre that he had been found.

The hospital suggested no visitors until 2 p.m. the following day, to allow his leg to be placed in plaster and for him to relax and to recover as far as possible from the hypothermia. She readily agreed and said she would drive over to Strensford tomorrow—there'd be no trouble getting time off work—and she thanked me for my swift action. I suggested she write to thank the Moors Search and Rescue team. The story did reach the local papers and Gordon's work as an artist was featured, the published story being that he had lost his footing while searching for suitable scenes to paint and had injured himself so severely in a fall that he could not climb from the gully. There was no reference to any domestic problems and none of the journalists highlighted the fact he'd had no painting materials with him when found.

I did visit Gordon in hospital and he was allowed home after three weeks with his leg in plaster and his future uncertain. When I called at the house in late May, he was working on the lawn, painting a picture of the reservoir waters which flooded the dale before him. The dam was in the background and I could see he had incorporated the newly added packhorse bridge and the two anonymous girls on bikes.

'She says it's all over between her and Ken,' he told me, as he roughly brushed some watery colouring to the sky section of his paper. 'But I don't believe it! He's been ringing, Nick, I know the signs. When I pick the phone up, he rings off.'

'Deirdre told me she would end the affair,' I tried to reason with him. 'I'm sure she has.'

'Has she? How can I be sure of that, Nick? The bloody man's working just a few yards down the lane, all day, every day, she has to pass him on the way to work and back from work ... how can she say it's all over?'

'She does love you,' I tried.

'And what a God-awful way of showing it!' he spat. 'Letting me down like that, my wife ...'

'Gordon, when you got lost on the moors, you didn't try to end it all, did you?' I felt I had to ask that question.

'End what? My life? No bloody fear. Nick, I want to get my own back on that man. I walked around for hours that day in pouring rain and thick fog, thinking about what he'd done to me. About what she'd done to me. All right, so I was not thinking straight, but it was foggy, Nick, that's how I came to fall. It was an accident, not an attempt at suicide. I'm not that sort of man.'

'Then you'll recover well, and I'm sure Deirdre loves you still.'

'That remains to be seen, Nick. She's all over me now, fussing and feeding me and caring for my injuries but I'm not sure it's finished. Not sure at all.'

'I think Deirdre will bring it to an end.' I defended her this time.

'Maybe she will, but what about him? Her fancy man on the dam. I hate it, Nick. I bloody well hate it ...'

'Hate what?' I asked.

'That!' And with his brush, he indicated

256

the reservoir and the dam. 'I hate it all, that dam, that reservoir. It's destroyed my life.' And he spat on the painting, his spittle landing on his image of the old pack-horse bridge.

10

These are much deeper waters than I had
  thought.
    Sir Arthur Conan Doyle (1859–1930)

Gordon's broken leg in its coat of thick white plaster considerably restricted his movements. Without the car, which he insisted Deirdre used for work instead of relying on lifts, his excursions to the moors were very limited. Deirdre was not at work all the time, however, and even though she offered on occasions to drive him and his equipment to his favourite work stations, he declined. He said he had no desire to paint. He did allow her to drive him to his lecturing commitments, however, and for this, she sometimes took time off work. He appeared to enjoy those outings because they got him away from the house and the reservoir, and he could meet with and talk to differing groups of people. After a time, however, and with his leg still in plaster, he announced he would resume work at home. He needed the money, for one thing, and so he launched into a hectic programme of painting the reservoir again and again as gradually its waters rose and expanded before him. Suddenly, he seemed obsessed with the reservoir and its changing appearance.

I spoke to Deirdre several times over those weeks, and once again, she assured me her affair with Ken Rigby was over. They had parted friends, however, there was no blazing row and although Ken had declared his love, Deirdre was firm in her resolve. She had come to fully realize the harm she was doing to Gordon and that had made her determined to end the matter.

She spent her time trying to prove to Gordon that she really loved him, trying to win back his confidence and his trust, nursing him and doing her best to encourage him to continue and expand his range of work. They slept in separate rooms because Gordon declared he could not touch her, saying that her body was tainted by her adulterous activities. In telling me all this, I was pleased she could confide in me and she was wise enough to appreciate that Gordon's forgiveness

258

would take a long, long time. But she was prepared to wait.

On one occasion, I encountered Deirdre in Aidensfield. She had taken her car to the garage to have a new tyre fitted and was whiling away her time on the village seat which overlooked the war memorial. I stopped for a chat and we decided to take a walk together to keep our conversation away from flapping ears. During our stroll towards the moors, during which I was clad in my full uniform, Deirdre did confide further in me, this time telling me about Gordon's very deep black moods. They were sometimes triggered by small matters and sometimes the result of greater stresses; sometimes they persisted for weeks and sometimes for a matter of hours. She did say this was one area of concern when Gordon had decided to give up his full-time job—she'd wondered how he would cope if things did not work out. She'd felt that any real pressure upon him, either financial or professional, would cause him to enter one of his periods of black depression but she had avoided that by giving him her total support. He'd avoided those deep moods until now and she said it was her foolishness that had triggered the current crisis. Although he was working again, she had no idea when he would completely return to normal.

As she'd watched him at work in recent days, repeatedly painting the same stormy picture of the reservoir, she could not say whether or not he had snapped out of it. The fact he was painting once more did suggest he had partially overcome that problem; the fact he was repeatedly painting the same scene and the reservoir in particular with its array of dark stormclouds, however, was perhaps an indication that all was not well with his state of mind. And he steadfastly refused to touch her body.

She did express an opinion that he'd been undergoing one of those moods, or perhaps it was the beginning of the current one, at the time he'd felt compelled to walk the moors on the day he was injured. He'd be brooding over what he regarded as a catastrophic period of his life, trying to work out a means of ending his agony or getting his revenge—and the fall had probably brought his broodings to an unexpected and painful end. As she took me into her confidence in this way, I asked, 'Deirdre, would Gordon do anything silly while he's in one of his dark moods?'

'It's always been at the back of my mind that he might,' she admitted.

'Like what?' I pressed her.

'I don't know,' she admitted. 'I don't know how far he'd go or what he'd do.'

'Suicide?' I asked. 'When you called me out the other week to look for him, did you think he might have decided to end his life?'

'It was something I'd considered, yes, but I daren't say so at the time,' she said. 'Somehow, I think he's either too timid or too sensible to end his own life, but, well, when a person's mind is disturbed, you've no idea what they might do. Gordon is fine until things go wrong, and then he seems to go deep into himself.'

'Sulking?' I smiled.

'No, it's worse than that. He broods inwardly. He becomes totally absorbed in his own world, preoccupied with things he never talks about, and has fits of black depression ...'

'Does he receive any help with this? Treatment of any kind?'

She shook her head. 'No, he refuses to recognize that he has an illness and let's face it, Nick, it always blows over and afterwards he's fine again. I've seen him have one of these moods for only an hour or so, and then it's all forgotten, but sometimes it can last longer.'

'How much longer?'

'Days, weeks.'

'Months?' I asked.

'It's possible, I suppose, although I've

never known one last more than two or three weeks.'

'But if a really serious problem arose, might it precipitate a long-term black mood in him?'

'Like my behaviour, you mean?' she asked.

'Yes,' I said.

'I suppose it could—that might be happening now, mightn't it? Is that what you are thinking?'

'I did have that in mind,' I admitted, following with, 'Has he ever harmed you?'

'No, never; he's not a violent person, Nick. He just goes very quiet and withdrawn. Usually, I leave him alone and he comes out of it full of apologies then goes off to paint a moody sort of picture full of black clouds and storms. By painting storms, he somehow gets it out of his system. But this time, it's different.'

'How's it different?' I put to her.

'I caused his anguish by deceiving him in the worst possible way,' she spoke quietly. 'It's the most dreadful thing I could have done to him, but it's over, Nick, honest. Now I have to convince Gordon and that's the difficult part. I'd say in his present mood, its impossible—he won't believe I've stopped seeing Ken. It might take me a long, long time, and a lot of patience, but I'll do it; I must, for his sake and mine.'

'He spat at his painting when I saw him recently; he said he hated the dam and the reservoir,' I told her. 'He didn't say he hated you.'

'He does blame the dam and the reservoir for making things go wrong,' she said. 'They brought Ken here, he once told me, and he hates them for that. Without the dam and the reservoir, there'd be no Ken, no affair with me ... that's how he sees it.'

'And he hates Ken?'

'He's never said that, Nick, but I'm sure he does. He thinks Ken deceived him too, you know, encouraging him to visit the site to paint those official pictures while seeing me behind Gordon's back.'

'So how do you read the present state of his mind?' I asked.

'I've no idea, he is very unsettled and uncommunicative; he will emerge from this mood, I know, and the fact he's painting again is encouraging. But it's my problem, Nick, I must sort it out.'

'I'll visit him when I'm in Ramsdale again,' I reminded her.

'Thanks. He's always looked forward to your visits and chats; he hasn't many close friends.'

'And you'll keep in touch?' I invited. 'If you need any help, don't be frightened to call.'

'Thanks, Nick. You're very kind.'

We had walked in a large circle and I continued my stroll with her, returning with her to the garage. Her car was ready, she thanked me, and drove away towards Ramsdale where Gordon would be waiting. I had a feeling he'd be checking on her movements, perhaps ringing the garage or the post office or some of his contacts in the village to find out where she was. I reflected on what she had told me and thought it might be advisable if Gordon sought psychiatric help but that had to come from his own desire to do so. No one could compel him to take that action. He was not certifiable, I felt; he was not the sort of person who should be locked up in an institution and yet, with modern medical advances, there might be some treatment from which he could benefit. I did ponder briefly upon his own sexuality, for I was aware they had no children although I did not know the reason. But, as Deirdre had said, all this was her problem or more truthfully, it was their joint problem. I could not and should not interfere.

Over the following weeks, Gordon painted and painted yet again the watery scene before him, sometimes incorporating the two nameless schoolgirls on bikes, and in that time, his leg mended, the plaster was removed and the water level in the reservoir rose yet further. It crept closer and closer to Gordon's house, filling what had once been a deserted dale and washing across what had recently been a sea of mud with aquatic birds making the most of their new environment.

Gordon painted it all, day by day, week by week—but whenever I paid him a visit, his pictures portrayed dark waters beneath black and stormy clouds. I wondered if he would ever paint a sunny scene but did not suggest it, nor did I ask why he persisted with his dark pictures.

As the reservoir was being slowly filled and the finishing touches were being made to the various buildings and structures which would serve it, I enjoyed frequent chats with Ken in his site hut. I did mention Deirdre and in return he did assure me that the affair was over—they had not fallen out, he stressed, but had mutually agreed after a long and very difficult conversation, that it was in everyone's best interest if he never saw her again. And, once again, I believed him.

During those chats, I was interested to know there had been no underground leaks, no water had permeated beneath the foundations, the dam itself had not shown any signs of leakage or weakness, and the ground which was now carrying the new lake had proven capable of acting as a giant container. Although the dam and reservoir were not quite complete, some of the work-force were leaving. Their part in the construction had been completed.

Gradually, their numbers reduced as the giant machines departed from the dale. But Ken remained in his site office. It was while the work-force was being reduced that I called again on Gordon and found him at work in his garden, painting yet another reservoir scene. This time it was different. It was a cheerful picture. He had incorporated some mallard and blackheaded gulls on the water and on this occasion the water was a beautiful blue. Its colour came from the reflection of the sky and there was not a black cloud in sight. I had no idea whether or not this was a significant moment in his life, but I did feel he had conquered that long, long mood of despair. He smiled when I arrived, made me a coffee as usual, and we settled down to enjoy it. He was happier and more relaxed than I had seen him for months. Deirdre was at work in the shop, he told me, and went on to say how she'd nursed him through his injuries with all the tender loving care she could muster. I did not question him any more about Deirdre's affair, thinking that any reference I might make would trigger off bad memories. I reasoned that if he wanted to discuss the matter, then he would raise it, but he didn't. We parted on that occasion just as we had done many times prior to, and indeed during, her liaison with Ken. It was almost as if there had been no intervening problem; Deirdre was at work, Gordon was producing his beautiful pictures, Ken was in his site office and I was performing my routine patrols. If there was one difference between now and those early days, it was that the dale now contained a massive but beautifully crafted dam behind which acres of water were spreading to provide a unique kind of serenity and beauty.

But things were not destined to remain like that.

As so often happens in such cases, the problems began almost accidentally. A combination of innocent circumstances produced a devastating effect. Gordon had been invited to be guest speaker at a ladies' luncheon club in Eltering. As with such cases, he was invited to join the group for the meal which began at 12.45 p.m. and then to speak for about three-quarters of an hour. He'd be paid a handsome fee and the ladies wanted some light-hearted tales of his life as a professional artist; he could also take a few pictures for display and possible purchase. This was the kind of outing he enjoyed. But because Deirdre was working at Sandra North's Fashions in Ashfordly, it was decided that Gordon, whose leg was now fully healed, should drive her there so that he could have use of the car. She finished work at 1 p.m. but had some shopping to do, so Gordon said he would collect her after his talk. His calculations were that if the meal began at 12.45 p.m. and continued for the anticipated hour and a half, he would begin his talk at 2.15 p.m. That meant he would conclude around 3 p.m. which in turn meant he'd arrive at Ashfordly to collect Deirdre around 3.30 p.m. He told her he'd park in Ashfordly market-place and she would seek the car. He didn't mind waiting if she was delayed, and likewise, she said she had enough to occupy her until he arrived, so he hadn't to worry about being late. Lunch followed by a speaker could never be guaranteed to finish at a specific time.

It seemed a very amicable arrangement and suggested their marriage crisis was healing. But Gordon's talk finished earlier than expected. Lunch had started absolutely on time with speedy clearance of the dishes between courses.

Another factor was that there were only two courses, not three, and so Gordon had found himself on his feet at 1.30 p.m. instead of the anticipated 2.15 p.m., and he had finished by 2.15 p.m. A few questions followed and even after time for a chat about the paintings he'd taken with him, and the sale of one of them, he left the hotel at 2.30 p.m. for the fifteen minute drive to Ashfordly. At 2.50 p.m. or thereabouts, he was easing to a halt in Ashfordly market-place, almost three-quarters of an hour earlier than either he or Deirdre had expected. I became aware of these timings due to the enquiries I had to make afterwards.

As he came to a halt, he sought Deirdre among the people who were thronging the place, but did not find her and consequently decided he'd buy a magazine from a newsagent's shop, then pop into a café for a cup of tea to pass the time. His talk had made him thirsty and the pubs were shut so a refreshing pint of beer was out of the question. But as he'd walked into Beckside Café, he was mortified to see Deirdre sitting at a table with Ken Rigby. They were enjoying tea and scones, laughing and talking to each other like old friends. For a moment, they did not see Gordon; he halted abruptly in the doorway, wondering what course of action to take, then slammed the door and stormed out. Deirdre heard the crash of the door and looked up to see her husband striding across the market-place

269

in what was clearly a very foul mood. He hurried towards his car, leapt in and slammed the door. As the engine burst into life, Deirdre came rushing out of the café running across to their car, but she was too late. Gordon roared out of the market-place with tears pouring down his face as Deirdre stood and stared at the departing vehicle.

Ken Rigby then appeared at her side and took her gently in his arms, saying he'd run her home. When she arrived home, Gordon was not there and neither was the car. That's when she rang me. I was on patrol at the time, having at that stage of my service been issued with a mini-van. Mary took the call, assessed its urgent nature and managed to have me contacted by radio from Ashfordly Police Station. Alf Ventress's distinctive voice came over the air.

'Urgent request to visit Ramsdale House, Nick, home of Mr and Mrs Precious who I believe are known to you. Mrs Precious is there now, Mr Precious has disappeared. She'd like you there as soon as you can make it.'

'Will co, Alf,' I responded. 'I'll submit a situation report as soon as I have established the nature of the problem.'

'Message understood, Control out,' he said, and ended the conversation.

When I arrived at Ramsdale House, Deirdre was in tears and was being comforted by Ken Rigby. He'd made a pot of tea and had lit the fire, and when I arrived, they were standing before it in misery.

'I'm so sorry, Nick, to bother you like this ...' She was weeping softly.

'What's happened?' I looked at both for some clarification.

Deirdre told me about that day's transport arrangements which had been made by Gordon, and said she'd gone into Beckside Café for a cup of tea to while away the moments until he arrived to collect her. By chance, Ken had been in the café, too, having already bought his snack; he'd spotted her and had invited her to share his table.

It was nothing more than that; it was not a planned meeting or a secret liaison. It was just how it had worked out. But Gordon had stumbled upon them, misreading the situation due to his early arrival. He'd stormed away without seeking for an explanation.

'I'm so miserable,' she sobbed. 'He'd forgiven me, at least I think he had. We were just getting together again, it was lovely, so lovely, with him loving me and sleeping with me, and working and producing those lovely pictures ... I

271

mean, how jealous can he get? It was just a cup of tea and chat with people all around ...'

'Where do you think he's gone?' I asked.

'I don't know.' She spread her hands in a gesture of defeat. 'I just don't know.'

'I might be able to get some lads from the site to help look,' offered Ken.

'I don't think my sergeant will sanction a full-scale search yet,' I had to tell them. 'A man driving off in his car after a row with his wife is hardly the sort of thing that justifies a search party.'

'But you know him, Nick.' She was almost pleading now. 'He could do anything.'

'If we think he might harm himself, then that could be justification for launching a full-scale search,' I said.

'I think he might ...' she whimpered.

'I'd have to tell my boss the whole story,' I warned her. 'He'll have to justify his actions to the search team which means I can't guarantee the searchers will not talk to the Press ...'

'I don't care!' She was weeping freely now. 'I just don't care, I just want him found.'

I took a detailed description of Gordon and his car, including its registration number, and then rang Sergeant Blaketon.

Reminding him of our earlier search for Gordon, I told him the story, stressing my belief that this time Gordon was likely to harm himself in some way, and suggesting that all patrols be given the car's number so that it might be located. He agreed with that course of action. He would not sanction a full-scale call-out of a search party because we had no starting point and no cause for thinking Gordon had made for the remoteness of the moors. He was with his car. We had to find that first. That was the most important because wherever it was discovered, it would provide a clue to his whereabouts. I hoped he had not decided to connect a hosepipe to the exhaust in an attempt to asphyxiate himself—we did come across lots of suicides on the moors who had taken that course.

I told Deirdre what we'd done. I said that every patrolling officer in the North Riding of Yorkshire, including those near our boundaries with the East Riding and in Middlesbrough Borough, had been supplied with Gordon's registration number. There was a distinct possibility the car would be found but I could not predict the state of Gordon's mind when we found him. I asked Ken if he would stay with Deirdre—he said he would, qualifying that remark by adding he would make sure he left the building before Gordon returned. I suggested he didn't answer the phone and hid his car somewhere!

Then I left, saying I would drive to the various vantage points with which I was familiar in the hope I could spot the car either on the heights or in the dales below. I carried some powerful binoculars to aid me; they were almost permanently in the vehicle and had proved their usefulness on many occasions. In spite of my search and in spite of knowing Gordon's car by sight, I did not find him. I kept in touch with Ashfordly Police Station by radio and asked Alf Ventress to ring Deirdre from time to time, to see if Gordon had made contact. But she'd not heard a thing from him, and by eight that evening, there was no sign of Gordon.

I was on duty until 10 p.m. but was prepared to work all night if necessary, and then just after nine o'clock, I received a radio call from Alf Ventress.

'Nick,' he said. 'We've had a call from George Dixon, the manager of Thackerston Quarry. Can you get yourself there as soon as possible? Sergeant Blaketon's *en route* and will rendezvous with you at the quarry. Someone's broken into the explosives store, it's happened since 5 p.m. this afternoon. They've taken a large quantity of explosives along with some detonators and fuses.'

11

Many waters cannot quench love,
neither can the floods drown it ...
The Song of Solomon viii.7

The explosives store at Thackerston Quarry
consisted of a small rectangular brick
building constructed especially for that
purpose. It was located on an elevated
portion of land some fifty yards from the
vast hollow in the limestone in which were
situated the various quarry faces. Out of
sight of casual visitors and passers-by, it
was securely built into an excavation in
the ground and had a thick concrete roof
above a metal-faced door secured with a
very stout padlock. There were no windows
and no markings by which its contents
might be known. A small sloping concrete
path led down to the single door—about
half the store's height was above ground
level. I knew it well because it was one of
several similar small explosives stores on
my beat. I had to inspect each of them
at least once every three months and, like
most of the others, this was classed as a

Mode A Registered Store, the mode being determined by its structure which in turn was determined by the quantity and type of explosives kept there.

I arrived at the quarry ahead of Sergeant Blaketon and found George Dixon in his office. He was a large, rather ungainly man in his late fifties and sported a big round face with an eternal smile below a head, bald save for a few wisps of grey hair. I asked him to take me to the store. He pressed a switch on his office whereupon a light on a tall post above the store floodlit the scene.

Armed with our torches, we walked across to the store. When I arrived, the door was standing wide open, but inside there were some cases of dynamite, fuses and detonators. Most had not been touched, the thief having taken only enough for his particular purpose.

'I didn't touch anything so you fellers could see how exactly the raider left it,' George said.

'Good thinking, George,' I thanked him. 'So what's gone?'

'Rolls of quarrying explosive, lengths of shot-firing cable, fuses that is, and fulminate of mercury detonators. He's taken thirty pounds of explosive—Amelite and Ammina makes, and enough fuses and detonators to set the whole lot off. He cut the hasp of the padlock with bolt cutters; the lock's on the ground where he left it.' His torch indicated the remains. 'A professional job, I'd say.'

'Not an opportunist crime?' I suggested.

'No, he came specially,' George was positive about that. 'If he'd parked his car anywhere near the quarry gates I'd have seen him or heard him. I reckon he parked out of my sight and beyond the range of my hearing, then came across country to the store. He knew where he was going, where the store was; it takes a bit of finding so he knew where to come. And you can climb our boundary fences easily enough.'

'So you're saying it's somebody who knew exactly what he wanted and where to find it?'

'I am,' said George with conviction.

'So why would anyone want to steal quarrying explosives?' I asked.

'To blow a bloody great hole in something,' he laughed. 'We use it for blasting rock. You could use it to blow up a tree stump or demolish a factory chimney or blast a hole in the ground to make a fish pond ...'

'Or open a safe?' I asked.

'There's enough here to blow up the Houses of Parliament,' he said.

'Guy Fawkes a suspect, is he?' I tried to make a joke of this.

'I wouldn't object to anybody blowing up Harold Wilson's government, those bloody Socialists have made a right mess of things like they always do,' George grinned. 'But I don't think chummy's taken this lot just to open a safe; he's taken enough to blow a big hole in something like the Bank of England.'

I examined the ground around the store but apart from the damaged remains of the lock, there was little of interest—the villain had left nothing incriminating and the concrete path did not show his footprints. I made a careful search over a wider area but did not find the bolt cutters, although I was limited by the darkness. A daylight search would be necessary but it did seem he'd taken the cutters with him. An examination of the ground which surrounded the store did not reveal any footprints either—it was too hard and dry, consequently I could not determine from which direction the thief had entered the quarry. Tomorrow's daylight search might show where he'd clambered over the surrounding fences or if he'd got caught on the barbed wire; there might be useful evidence like fibres from his clothing or footprints and tyre marks in some softer earth.

'How would be carry it away?' was my next question.

'One man could easily carry all that that's gone.' he affirmed. 'A sack mebbe, bag of some sort, suitcase even. The lot wouldn't weigh more than a small sack of taties and it won't explode by being bumped about. It needs fuses and detonators.'

'So what prompted you to check the store?' I asked. 'Did you hear noises or something?'

'No. It's summat I allus do at night,' George told me. 'We stopped work at half-four and I did my usual closing-down rounds when everybody had gone. The store was locked—we keep it locked until we need access as you know. I checked the store about five o'clock, summat I do every day. It was OK then, locked and secure.'

'You inspected it personally?' I had to ask.

'Aye, I did. Then I usually have a walk around at night after supper, before I go to bed.'

George lived in the manager's cottage which was part of the quarry complex. A check of the quarry each night would take him only a few minutes and I knew he was a diligent employee of the company who owned it. Making such checks would be something he would do with great care.

'So you didn't hear a car or anything?' I asked. 'Notice people about?'

He shook his head. 'No, nowt. I just did my rounds as usual and found it like it is now. The minute I saw what had been done, I rang your office and waited for you fellers to get here.'

As we chatted, Sergeant Blaketon arrived, parked his car outside George's office and spotted us beneath the powerful light which illuminated the store. He emerged from the car, put on his cap and made his way towards us.

'So Rhea,' he said, when he arrived slightly out of breath after the modest climb. 'What's happened?'

I briefed him on the situation as provided by George. He asked when I had last checked the store and I told him it had been ten days earlier; I added that during my routine night and early-morning patrols I hadn't noticed any suspicious vehicles or trespassers near the quarry gates. I hadn't had any reason to suspect someone was planning this raid or that the store had been previously targeted, and George confirmed this view.

Living so close to the quarry, he was in an ideal position to see or hear trespassers, but had never encountered any. Tonight's raid had therefore come as a total surprise. I picked up the damaged lock and told George I was retaining it as evidence, hopefully in the

280

event of us catching the perpetrator. If we did, and if we found the cutters he'd used, the marks they'd left upon the hasp might be identifiable. I itemized the stolen explosives and their accessories, listing the manufacturer's names and markings, and said we would immediately circulate a description to all our stations, both locally and nationally.

With some luck on our part, and bearing in mind George had discovered the crime very soon after it had been committed, we might find the thief still in possession of the explosives. I knew our night patrols would be constantly alert.

George had a spare padlock and so he secured the store and said he would now notify his superiors. I would drive to Ashfordly Police Station to record the crime and circulate details, and I would commence my enquiries immediately.

'And when you've completed your crime report, Rhea,' said Blaketon. 'Get yourself around all the other stores on your beat. Check them all before you go off duty. Let's hope no more have been done. I'll instruct your night-duty colleagues to do likewise when they come on duty. We'll check all explosives stores in our section overnight. It looks as if you'll be working overtime!'

'Very good, Sergeant,' I said.

I had intended working late anyway, in an attempt to trace Gordon, but I did not think this theft would add greatly to my hours of duty. There were not many such stores on my patch—only three—and I was able to visit each before I would normally have booked off duty. But I almost overlooked a fourth. It was at the reservoir site. They did have a small store which, in the early stages of the work had contained a substantial amount of explosives but which was now fulfilling a much more reduced role as the work was nearing completion. There was very little blasting to be done at this stage. I had enough time for a brief visit to the site before finishing this tour of duty. When I arrived, Ken Rigby had gone home but the night security guard responded to the bell which I rang at the gate.

'Evening, Constable.' He was a stout little man with a black moustache beneath a dark peaked cap. I thought he looked like Adolf Hitler and noticed he did not offer to unlock the gate to admit me.

I realized he was going to make me stand outside for our conversation. For the moment, I was prepared to accept that, at least until I had explained the reason for my presence. Then I wanted to be let in.

'Evening.' I did not know his name but

felt such details did not matter. 'I'm here to tell you that an explosives store has been raided at Thackerston. Some rolls of quarrying explosive have gone, with detonators and fuses. The raid was some time after five o'clock this evening. So I'm here to make sure your store is secure.'

'It is,' he said firmly. 'I've checked it. It's one of my regular jobs. I check it every hour on the hour. And I make an entry in my duty log to that effect. Very keen on such things is this company. And so am I.'

'I'd like to see it,' I said.

'I've orders not to admit nobody once the main gate is locked.' He did not smile but studied me through the thick wire mesh. 'And that means nobody.'

I felt like telling him that 'not to admit nobody' meant he had to admit everybody but he wouldn't have understood the full import of making use of the double-negative in such a way.

'I have a statutory duty to inspect all explosives stores on my beat,' I said. 'That is why I am here. If you do not admit me, I shall report you for obstructing a constable in the execution of his duty. And that will mean a court appearance and if you are convicted, which you would be, then you'd have difficulty getting another job in security. You'd be a man with a criminal record.'

'There's no need to take that attitude!' he bristled.

'I think there is, seeing as you are being very obstructive,' I grinned. 'So, how about letting me in?'

With some misgivings, therefore, he admitted me, locked the gate in my wake and led me through the site to the store. Similar in construction to that at Thackerston Quarry, I was pleased to note that it was secure and made a note in my pocket book to that effect.

'See? I said it was all right,' he muttered.

'So you did, but I had to see it for myself. That's my duty. Now, is everything else all right?' I asked this Black Adolf.

'Are you checking up on me?'

'No, why should I want to do that?'

'So what else do you want to see?' he almost snarled.

'Nothing,' I smiled at him. 'This is your responsibility, not mine. But I like to know if there's been any problems of a criminal nature ... it's something I always ask when I visit this site.'

'Nowt apart from them bolt cutters,' he grunted.

'What bolt cutters?' I asked with considerable interest.

'Them what's been missing since this afternoon,' he said. 'They told me when I came on. They didn't think nobody from

284

outside's nicked 'em; more like somebody what's working here 'as taken 'em home I shouldn't wonder, to do some cutting job at home. They asked me to look out for 'em in case they're lying about the place. Went missing from the tool store, they did.'

'They've not been reported to the police, have they?' I asked.

'Now how can I know the answer to that?' he grunted.

'Because you are a security man. I thought you might have known the answer. But I am interested in them.'

If the theft of the bolt cutters had been reported to any police station or officer, I would have known, so it seemed the company had dealt internally with the matter. But in this case, there was an added factor. I decided not to elaborate the reason for my interest but when I asked if he could describe the bolt cutters, he said he could not. All he'd been told was that a pair of bolt cutters were missing and he'd been asked to watch out for them on his nightly rounds. They could be lying anywhere on site.

So, I asked myself, did we have a site worker who was stealing explosives, or did we have someone who had managed to gain access to the site and who had stolen the cutters specifically to gain entry to the Thackerston explosives store? The two incidents might not be connected but in the realms of criminal investigation, such coincidences could be rarely discounted. If bolt cutters were missing from the reservoir site since this afternoon and a pair had been used to steal explosives less than five miles away, then a link of some kind was highly feasible.

I had to talk to Ken Rigby about the bolt cutters and guessed he would still be with Deirdre Precious at her home; apart from that, I had to make a final check to see if Gordon had returned or left any messages and so I drove the short distance from the site to Ramsdale House.

The entire place was illuminated like a lighthouse and when I knocked, Deirdre came to the door, tearful and harassed.

'Any news?' she asked, even before I was admitted.

I shook my head. 'Sorry, not a sighting. All our patrols are searching right now and when the night shift comes on, they'll continue until dawn.'

Ken appeared in the doorway behind her; he was clutching a glass of whisky and heard my comments.

'Anything I can do?' he asked.

'Not really, but I'm here on another matter,' I said.

His face adopted a worried appearance

and I wondered what else he might have been up to, in addition to his liaison with Deirdre. But, I reasoned, a lot of people look guilty when a police officer suggests they've been wrongdoing! I was invited in and given a mug of coffee whereupon I explained about the theft of the explosives and the use of the bolt cutters. I concluded with, 'I called at your site a few minutes ago for a chat with Black Adolf, and he said you'd mislaid some cutters today.'

'We have, but I didn't want the police involved; it's an internal matter, Nick, it happens all the time. We get stuff nicked by the work-force, sometimes they fetch it back, sometimes we write it off. If we rang you every time something was stolen, you'd never be away from the place. So are you saying our cutters were used for that job?'

'I'm saying bolt cutters were used, and we know you've lost some. Would yours cut through the hasp of a security padlock?'

'No problem. They'll cut anything from iron bolts to chicken wire by way of nails, screws and wire washing lines! Wonderful tools.'

'If yours turn up, can you let me know?' I asked him. 'And if we find any bolt cutters thrown away after that explosives raid, can we show them to you? I'll be searching the scene in daylight. You've no men with you, have you, who might resort to nicking bolt cutters and then explosives?'

'Not to my knowledge, Nick. If it was one of our staff, you'd think they'd have raided our own store, wouldn't you? We haven't much there, but there's enough left to blow a useful hole in the ground.'

'That makes sense. OK, but if the cutters turn up on site, could you let me know?'

'Sure, but why?'

'We can do forensic tests to see if they were used for shearing that lock, and there might be prints on the handles too.'

'Fair enough. I'll call you, Nick. And I hope you didn't upset our guardian angel!'

'The Prince of Darkness, you mean? I upset him no more than he upset me,' I grinned. After reassuring Deirdre that we were doing everything we could to trace Gordon, and asking her to ensure she called Ashfordly Police Station the moment she heard anything from him, I departed. I decided to go home and have some supper; as Mary would be expecting me home at 10 p.m. she'd have a meal ready and I decided to make use of it to sustain me through the night's extra work.

Before going home, though, I drove to

Ashfordly Police Station to update Sergeant Blaketon about the bolt cutters and he said he would incorporate that additional information in our crime circulars. Also, I told him there'd been no word from the missing Gordon.

I went home for my quick meal, thinking that in addition to keeping an eye open for Gordon, I'd be wondering where I might find the abandoned bolt cutters and/or the stolen explosives. As I talked over my day's activities with Mary while enjoying the hefty supper which might have to sustain me all night, I found myself admiring one of Gordon's paintings on my kitchen wall.

I'd bought it some months ago and it showed a dark view of the reservoir overcast with dense black clouds. It was then I remembered Gordon's words. He'd said, 'I hate it all, that dam, that reservoir … it's destroyed my life.'

And as I recalled his venom as he spat upon his own painting, I realized Gordon might want to destroy the dam, the reservoir and all they represented.

12

To be, or not to be: that is the question:
Whether 'tis nobler in the mind to suffer
The slings and arrows of outrageous fortune,
Or to take arms against a sea of troubles,
And by opposing end them?

William Shakespeare (1564–1616)

For a few minutes, I was unsure of my own suspicions but the more I considered the possibility, the more I realized Gordon could be planning to destroy the dam. Being the contractor's official artist, he did have ready access to the site which meant he'd be familiar with the layout as well as the location and purpose of the various temporary buildings. In addition, he'd know something about the security system such as the time Black Adolf had his breaks. Gordon's presence on the site, even during a mid-afternoon, would not be unusual which meant he could have had an opportunity to sneak into the tool shed to remove the bolt cutters. And if he'd been carrying his easel and painting gear at the time, he would have been able to conceal the cutters among his belongings. It would have been much more difficult, however, to have raided the site's explosives' store while people were around—that's if he knew of its presence.

It was while contemplating that scenario, that I recalled he'd worked in the Rural District Council offices, one of his responsibilities being licensing.

Local authorities were responsible for various licensing matters under a number of statutes ranging from horse-riding establishments and refreshment houses to hackney carriages by way of pet shops, keepers of petroleum spirit, theatres and more. Although the police issued explosives licences and certificates, the range of local authority licensing responsibilities did include the general administration of the provisions of the Explosives Act, 1875 and the Control of Explosives Order, 1953. It meant Gordon would know the locations of all existing local explosives stores and their likely contents but he might have been unaware of the reservoir store because it was so recent. It might not have been installed while he was still working for the council.

I could add to these considerations my theory that Gordon would not have disposed of the cutters after severing the padlock at Thackerston because he'd need them later; he'd want them to cut a hole through the wire fence around the reservoir site so he could gain access to the dam compound under cover of darkness when Black Adolf was otherwise engaged. For a few minutes, I sat with my mug in my hand, staring at the picture on the wall as if in a trance, then Mary nudged me and asked, 'Are you all right?'

'I've just realized who's nicked those explosives and what he's going to do with them!' I whispered hoarsely.

'Who?' she asked.

'Gordon Precious!' I said, with a brief explanation of my reasoning.

'Surely, even if his wife had gone off with that foreman, he wouldn't blow up the new dam, would he?' She was incredulous at my suggestion. 'He's not that sort of person, surely?'

'I'm not happy with the state of his mind,' I spoke quietly. 'So put it this way, now that I've aired my thoughts, would you risk doing nothing to find him?'

'So what can you do? You don't know where he is!'

'I think I know where he's heading with his bagful of stolen quarry explosives. I've got to find him and stop him!' I said, rushing to the telephone.

I rang Sergeant Blaketon and explained my theories. He listened intently and agreed with my reasoning, saying, 'Right, Rhea, get yourself over to Ramsdale. Find that foreman and tell him, then wait for me. I'll have to inform the duty inspector at Sub-Division, and then give me time to rustle up as many constables as I can at short notice. And I think we'd better adopt a softly-softly approach, no blue lights and blaring sirens. We don't want to panic him into doing something even more stupid than he intends.'

'Right, Sergeant.'

'We've got to search that place, the entire dam and reservoir complex, and we've got to stop Precious, otherwise Aidensfield will finish up as a sea of mud with God knows how many deaths ... it's imperative we find him, Rhea! See if the foreman, what's his name ...?'

'Rigby,' I said.

'Yes, see if Rigby can muster some helpers as well. There is an emergency plan for problems on the site, we discussed it when I first called on him.'

'Right, Sergeant,' I said.

'And don't do anything stupid before I get there!' he grunted, before slamming down the telephone. I rang Deirdre Precious's home number and asked to speak to Ken Rigby. After saying there'd been no word from Gordon, she handed the phone to him.

'Ken,' I said. 'Listen carefully. We need your help. We think Gordon raided that explosives store I mentioned earlier; if it is him, he's taken some fuses and detonators too. We think he's got your bolt cutters as well, and I reckon he's going to try and blow up your dam. You don't have to ask why!'

'Oh my God!' he almost screamed. 'That man must be mad ... it's nearly full—if that lot gets away you can say goodbye to most of your village. Right, what can we do?'

'I'm going to the site now,' I said. 'I'll meet you there in, say, fifteen minutes? Can you arrange as many site workers as possible, to help us search the site for Gordon? And for the explosives. Wait for our officers to arrive. We mustn't alarm Gordon, we might precipitate his actions. We need a softly-softly approach. Ask them to assemble outside the site and wait for us. In the meantime, can you think of all the places he might place the explosives to gain maximum effect? We need to search those places first. Get everyone there as soon as possible; if you've any explosives experts, bring them along.'

'Right.'

'And my sergeant is bringing as many

police as he can muster at short notice
...'

'Gordon shouldn't be able to get into the site at night,' said Ken.

'Consider that he might already be there, hiding and waiting. He might have got in earlier. Besides, if what I think is true, and if Gordon's really determined, do you think Black Adolf could really stop him?'

'Put like that, no. Right, Nick. I'll put our emergency plan into action. Should Deirdre stay here?'

'For the time being, yes. We need her near the telephone.'

'He won't blow up his house, will he?' asked Ken.

'Point taken. We'll have it searched and we'll put a guard on Deirdre.'

And I rushed out of the house not knowing what time I would return.

As I approached the site, Ken Rigby was waiting at the main gate which was now standing open. A powerful light shone from a tower above his head, bathing the ground about the gate in its pale white light and I noticed that a handful of men—half a dozen or so—surrounded him. Standing just inside the entrance was Black Adolf, the security man, while inside the tall wire fence were the site buildings, machines and the other accoutrements of this major construction project. And in the dark distance was the looming shape of the mighty dam, parts of it bathed in security lights and others in complete darkness.

It seemed to stretch away into the unseen distance but from here, I could not see any of the water that lapped gently behind it. I eased my mini-van to a halt and climbed out.

'Thanks Ken,' I said as I approached him. 'Anything happened?'

'Nothing. I've said nothing to anyone yet. I thought it best to wait.'

'What about the fence? Has it been breached?'

'I don't know, I haven't had it checked yet. I can do it now,' he said.

'There's no way of checking without making a tour of the entire boundary, is there?' I put to him.

'Sorry, no, we didn't go in for electrification. It means doing a visual check and there's more than a mile of high-wire fencing.'

'It'll have to be done as soon as possible,' I stressed. 'We have to know if Gordon's managed to get inside and if so, where he's likely to be. It would be beneficial if we could complete this check without alerting him.'

'My lads can do that, they know their way around and the darkness should provide a lot of cover. Do you want to brief them?'

Black Adolf and four other men raised their hands when I asked for volunteers, each saying they were familiar with the layout of the site and I asked them to check every inch of the boundary fence for signs of a hole big enough to admit a man accompanied by a load of explosives and, if possible, to examine the ground to see if he'd left any sign of his route once inside. There might be footprints.

I told them we'd not found his car but doubted if he'd be able to drive it close to the fence at any point other than the main gate. If he had taken it off road, there might be tracks in the earth, but finding those would be extremely difficult. Having been briefed, they understood the need for caution but I felt Black Adolf would be better employed at the main gate; I suggested he remain at the gate to act as liaison officer and that the rest of us adjourned to the site office to await the arrival of Sergeant Blaketon.

Blaketon with seven officers rapidly recruited from current night patrols and comprising two car loads arrived within quarter of an hour and I explained to him my actions so far. Even as we were conferring, the four searchers arrived to say they had found a large cut in the boundary fence. It was on the western section and comprised a vertical slash in the wire. The hole was some six feet tall and the strong wire had been folded back to make a large entrance hole, certainly big enough to admit a fully grown man and whatever he might be capable of carrying.

'Right,' said Sergeant Blaketon, as he assumed command. 'We need to make a detailed search of the site and of the ground near the gap, for footprints which might provide us with the direction he's taken. Mr Rigby, can we close and lock the main gate now? All the police officers immediately available have arrived; we could use your security man's services too. And I'd appreciate a plan of the site. If he's hiding, we want to know where to search.'

From the office next door, Ken obtained a site plan for Sergeant Blaketon to study, then went off to secure the gates and bring Black Adolf into the party.

By the time they returned, Blaketon had formulated his plans, dispatching one constable to guard Deirdre at Ramsdale House and another to guard the hole in the fence, in case the trespasser used it as an escape route. With everyone present, Sergeant Blaketon addressed us.

'Quite clearly, our immediate priority is the dam,' he said, after telling the group about Gordon and the stolen explosives. 'We will search in teams of two—one site worker to accompany one police officer. There are dangers as you can all appreciate but we must bear in mind the scenario if the dam does burst. I'm not sure what kind of timescale is involved but we need to complete our task with the minimum of delay and the utmost care. If the dam is found to be safe and if we find that no explosives are hidden upon or near it, we will place two constables in positions to maintain that state. If that is the case, it means Gordon could be elsewhere on the site, probably preparing whatever he has decided to do. Never forget he has the means of blowing himself up, or us, or anything else he might have in his mind. I cannot stress too strongly that the man is dangerous and that our time is necessarily limited. But I want no heroics ... Now, here is the dam,' and he pointed to a scale drawing which Ken had secured to the wall of the office. 'It is a large structure as you can see and every inch must be scrutinized. Mr Rigby, you're the one to guide us to the most vulnerable sites.'

Ken showed us, on the plan, the most vulnerable locations while explaining it would be most difficult to conceal any explosives either in or upon the face of the newly finished dam. The closely knit stone and concrete work did not permit it. Even to place explosives beneath the base, the most likely place for such an attack, was impossible although a powerful blast close to the base might produce some structural weakness.

Someone unaccustomed to the use of explosives might believe the base of the dam was the most suitable place to wreak severe damage and so every inch of the baseline would be scrutinized. Whether the amount stolen would cause a breach of the dam at the base was something Ken could not tell us—not without knowing the cumulative power of the explosives missing from the quarry. In fact, this dam was particularly well built, with sturdy foundations and a base which was far wider than its height, and that provided it with a very high degree of safety. Its base should resist an attack of the kind expected from Gordon but there were other vulnerable points. He could not take chances—he had no idea what knowledge Gordon had picked up during his painting visits to the site. He suggested several places which were at high risk, some close to sluices and the transformer. As we embarked upon our search, we detailed one constable to man the telephones and Black Adolf to act as liaison officer on the site.

Before leaving the site office, all the

teams were equipped with powerful hand searchlights drawn from the site store and Ken was also able to supply each team with walkie-talkie radio sets. Two constables with two site workers were allocated to the western edge of the base of the dam and one constable with one site worker to the western edge of the summit of the dam. An identical scheme was effected for the eastern end of the dam and all would work towards the centre.

Sergeant Blaketon remained in overall command with a roving commission and a radio set, and I was partnered with Ken, our task being to examine the powerhouse and the buildings which housed the transformer while Ken kept in constant touch with everyone over his radio. The first search proved negative. No trespassers were found within the boundaries of the site or on the dam itself, and there was no sign that the structure had been tampered with in any way. Gordon had not been found there; likewise, my search of the powerhouse and transformer buildings proved negative. Ken knew all the places which might have accommodated explosive material, but none was found.

Positioning one constable at each end of the dam to maintain security, Sergeant Blaketon next organized a second search of all the site buildings and offices, with particular attention to the spaces beneath them and to lofts, cupboards and storerooms, but nothing was found. Apart from the gaping hole in the perimeter fence, there was no indication that anything untoward had happened. In spite of that suspicious hole, I began to wonder if I had been grossly mistaken. Anxious to resolve the matter, I told Sergeant Blaketon I would ring Deirdre to see if she'd heard anything from Gordon.

I rang her from the site office but she said Gordon had not been in touch, neither had she heard or seen anything of his car. She thanked us for providing a guardian constable and said she would ring us at the site office if Gordon did make contact.

'He's still missing,' I told the searchers who had now been reassembled.

Blaketon turned to Ken. 'Mr Digby.' He adopted his most formal attitude, probably due to the fact that Ken's behaviour was partially responsible for this drama. 'My own instinct is that Gordon has either been on site to plant his bombs and left, either with or without an intention of returning to blow up the dam, or that this was a reconnaissance trip with the intention of returning at some future time to implement his plan. That might even mean later tonight. That hole in the fence does suggest some unauthorized person has entered. Or, of course, we might be barking right up the wrong tree altogether. Maybe Gordon is not coming here at all, maybe he did not raid the quarry explosives store and maybe he has no intention of harming the dam or anything connected with it. Remember, we have no evidence to support our theories, it's all conjecture. Our search has revealed nothing but I must ask you this—is there anywhere on this site, particularly within the vicinity of the dam, where a man could conceal himself?'

Ken shook his head. 'We've looked in all the likely hiding places and positions of vulnerability, they're all listed on our plans for easy reference and my lads know this place inside out, Mr Blaketon. He's not here and neither is that explosive. I'd guarantee that. And there were no footprints leading from that hole in the fence.'

'That's not surprising, the ground is covered with grass just there,' I pointed out.

Blaketon regarded me with an expression that could imply that I was little more than a nuisance, said, 'Rhea, you realize you could be wrong about all this?'

I did not know how to respond. I was very aware that my theory had resulted in this emergency turnout of police officers and site workers but equally, I knew we'd had no alternative. Gordon and a quantity of quarry-blasting explosives were missing. Those were two inescapable facts. Although there was no real evidence to link one incident with the other, the coincidence was too great to ignore. In addition, I'd heard Gordon express his hatred for the dam. And I'd seen his venom; if Gordon's state of mind was deeply disturbed, he would not be responsible for his actions. That made him very dangerous.

'I don't think we should leave the site.' I made my stand for what I believed was the right action. 'If he did make that hole in the fence, he might be here now, hiding and waiting for us to leave, or he might come back. Either way, we must stay and keep looking.'

'And how long do you suggest we all hang about, Rhea?' asked Blaketon. 'All night?'

Again, I hesitated then said, 'Until we find Gordon Precious,' I said. 'Dead or alive.'

'His car had not been found before I left the office,' he said.

'If he used it to come to the reservoir after his raid on the quarry and did not want it to be spotted,' I said, 'he would take it on to the moors, well off any formal road, and walk here. We'd never find it during a normal search. It could be on the moors above us now, a few hundred yards away, and we'd never see it in the darkness. Even in daylight, it would be most difficult to find without a bit of luck on our side.'

'Are you suggesting we search those moors?' was his next question.

'No, they're too vast and isolated, especially at night. I'm just making a point. I'm saying his car could be very close to us at this moment, which means he could be nearby too. With his explosives.'

'So, as the man on the spot, what is your next suggestion, Rhea?' He looked me directly in the eyes.

'That we undertake another very thorough search and that we maintain our presence on site, that we do it in an unobtrusive manner, that we continue to guard the dam and that our available night patrols continue to look out for Gordon's car—and for Gordon, just in case he is nowhere in this vicinity.'

'All right, let's do another search,' Blaketon sighed. 'And this time, we all change partners and we search a different place. No one should search the place they searched earlier. Right? Think—where, on this site, would a crazy man hide himself and a bag full of explosives?'

This time, I found myself with a middle-aged pipe-smoking site worker called Joe and because we had to concentrate yet again on the base of the dam, our allotted search area was the eastern end. When we were dispatched to our duties, I followed him to the extremity, the idea being to work towards the central concrete-built section from where the water issued under control to form the new stream. If there was a weak spot, that might be there, but that had been searched once—and would be searched again.

At ground level, we could physically inspect every nook and cranny aided by the torches we'd been given and by the arc lights which bathed most of the dam in their brilliant glow. But higher on the facing wall, we'd have to rely to some extent on the beams of our torches, pointing them high and sweeping their beams along the strong concrete and stone structure in the hope we might find the evidence we sought. But Gordon could never climb the smooth face of the dam to place his bomb in a crevice or crack—not that we found any such holes. In many ways, it was a forlorn hope. The overpowering darkness when away from the lights being our enemy and while it concealed our activities from Gordon, it did not make life any easier for the searchers.

Joe and I found ourselves below the huge face of the dam, where, on the land side, there was a careful blending of the steep slopes of the dale with the massive hewn stones. Each stone was some eight feet long by four feet deep and four feet thick; they had been rescued from a bridge demolition in Greece and were similar to those used in the construction of east-coast piers and sea-defences. Their dark, natural colouring, in some cases adorned with mossy growths, was a perfect match for the heathery slopes into which they would soon merge. Indeed, these huge stones already appeared a natural part of the hillside, a design success, whereas towards the centre, the dam's lofty concrete section looked pale and white in the lights.

I shone my torch skywards, allowing the powerful beam to sweep those rocks but knowing that no one was going to find any recess there into which to place any explosives.

You'd never find a hole big enough to admit a glass marble let alone a roll of quarry-blasting explosive. Nonetheless, I swept the beam of my powerful torch along the entire face of the dam and as the extended beam wavered, it highlighted the reconstructed Ramsdale Bridge on the eastern end of the dam, directly above me. The old stone pack-horse bridge with its distinctive arch now straddled the narrow walkway which ran along the top of the dam. Now a mere decorative feature rather than a functional bridge, its arch was high enough to admit a small car and certainly people could walk beneath it, but no one could walk or drive over it now.

I swept my beam along the end of the bridge which faced me, marvelling that the builders had managed to replace every stone in its former precise position. The end of the old bridge merged perfectly with the stonework below and I noted the shadow cast by the bridge. A dark oblong shadow was directly beneath the end of the bridge as I examined it—oddly enough, it was the exact shape and size of one of those mighty rectangular stones. Then I realized it wasn't a shadow. It was a huge hole ... and I remembered what it was!

It was the intended grave of Warwick Humbert Ravenswood. Situated on the highest level of stones, it would be above the water-line at the far side and thus not be subjected to any pressure from the water. Furthermore, it was secure from gawping tourists and likely vandals—and it would not be shown on Ken Rigby's scale plans of the site. In his search, he'd forgotten about it! From the path along the top of the dam, it would be invisible because the supports of the old bridge came down to the dam's road at that very place.

Once Warwick's burial had been completed and a covering stone placed at the entrance, it would be concealed, but currently it was the sort of place an artist would notice, especially if he was making a painting of the face of the dam. I wondered if it was possible to gain entry without erecting scaffolding or dangling rope ladders over the rails? I felt that any truly determined person could do so ... you'd crawl through the railings, hang on to them for dear life and swing the legs into the gaping space.

Even if a climber fell from there, the dam's face was sloping outwards so the faller would roll down and be cushioned by heather and bracken on the steep hillside into which the stonework merged. They'd escape serious injury, unlike a fall from the central portions which overlooked the concrete platform which carried the overflow into the rocky bed of Ramsdale Beck. Then I remembered how Gordon had entertained me with tales of rock-climbing in the Lake District ... to gain access to that hole would be comparatively easy for a proficient rock-climber!

It was the only hole in the dam that had not been searched. I radioed for Sergeant Blaketon.

13

Peace is in the grave. The grave hides all
   things ...
   Percy Bysshe Shelley (1792–1822)

There was no reply from Sergeant Blaketon's radio. Either the set was malfunction-
ing or he was out of range, so I called Ken
Rigby.

'Ken, it's Nick here. I think I know
where Gordon is. Can you join me at the
pack-horse bridge as soon as possible? With
a rope that will bear my weight? And before
you come, can you ring Deirdre and get her
to come to the pack-horse bridge.'

'Will co,' said Ken with quiet dignity
and without wasting time asking questions.

With my colleague Joe, I scrambled up
the steep side of the dale, using shrubs and
bracken to haul my way to the top and
then, panting with the exertion, I found
myself level with the walkway which ran
across the top of the dam. Followed closely
by the puffing Joe, I clambered over the
new metal railings and ran back towards
the pack-horse bridge. Although water was

roaring nearby, I put my finger to my lips to indicate silence from Joe as we padded beneath the old bridge. Standing beneath its curved arch, we both waited for a few moments to regain our breath and then, again stressing the need for silence, I walked to the railings standing as close as I could to the support of the pack-horse bridge, and peered over. I was looking into a huge hollow in the moors, with a stream rippling through from beneath the base of the dam. The whole area was bathed in a sea of bright light but blackened in patches by intense darkness.

From this vantage point, I was looking down the steep slope comprised of those mighty blocks of granite. Joe joined me. Without speaking, I indicated the patch of darkness directly below the end of the old bridge; from here, it was easy to see that it was a large hollow, a place destined to be the final resting place of Warwick Humbert Ravenswood but neither of us could say whether or not the hole contained anyone or anything. The angle prevented us from seeing inside. Looking from here, it would be just possible for a man to climb over the iron rails, cling to them as he found a foothold and then move to his right and slip into the cavity. Or he might have used a rope looped over the rails and around his own waist so that he could lower himself down the stonework, quite feasible for a rock-climber. But if a rope had been used, it had gone—which meant it would be most difficult if not impossible to return via the same route. And that thought sent a shiver down my spine. Or, of course, he was not there at all!

Unable to surreptitiously determine whether or not the cavity was occupied, we returned to the end of the dam to await the others. Here, thanks to the roar of the sluice, we could talk without worrying about the possible occupant of the cavity overhearing us and soon Ken arrived with a rope, closely followed by Deirdre. I explained the situation and asked them to be patient with us, and also to be as silent as possible. I did suggest to Ken and Deirdre that, if we located Gordon, he must not see them together. Then Sergeant Blaketon and some of the others arrived, having learned of this development, and I briefed them.

'So, Rhea, what are your plans?' Sergeant Blaketon asked.

'I'll call to him from the walkway and if there's no response, I'll lower myself on this rope and have a look into the cavity.'

'There's no other way of examining it, is there?' Blaketon addressed Ken who shook his head.

'Sorry, Sergeant, not at such short notice. We could build something especially for this task from ground level, using scaffolding, but that'll take ages. We've got that lined up for Warwick's funeral—I don't think the vicar's too happy about having to perform on a platform suspended in mid-air but we've had no complaints from Warwick.'

And so the decision was made. It was agreed that I should make the attempt because of my relationship with Gordon and Sergeant Blaketon thought I'd cope because I'd been on an Outward Bound course. With a round turn and two half hitches, I lashed one end of the rope to the railings, locating it as close as possible to the support of the pack-horse bridge, and tied the other around my waist in a bowline. The bowline is a knot which does not slip—so I would not slice my waist in half with my own weight! That completed, I would lower myself down the face of the dam until I could swing myself to the right and either gain access to the cavity or inspect it with a torch. But first, I had to call to see if Gordon was there.

From the railings, therefore, I called his name while the others, including Deirdre remained silent in the background. I called several times but there was no response.

'It looks as if you'll have to use your rock-climbing skills, Rhea,' whispered Blaketon, who added, 'Good luck—and watch out for bombs! Remember we don't want any heroics ...'

I didn't tell him I had no rock-climbing skills although I'd done a little abseiling but I saw no danger in what I was about to do. The base of the cavity was but a few feet below the walkway and I would be secured by the rope. Taking a deep breath, therefore, I climbed over the rails with my back to the dale beyond, took a secure grip of my rope and walked backwards down the slope of the heavy rocks. Within a few strides. the gaping hole of Warwick's grave-to-be was on my right. Holding the rope tightly, I bent my knees and then sprang out from the face of the dam, swinging to the right as I did so. With startling suddenness, I found my feet landing just inside the cavity, so I bent my knees and was thus partially inside it. And there was Gordon.

Even in the dim reflected light, I could see him—and my arrival startled him.

'God!' he gasped.

'Gordon, it's me, Nick Rhea,' I spoke quickly.

'Get away, leave me ...' His voice was faint and hoarse. 'I want to die ...'

Hauling the torch from my pocket and

hanging there with one hand on the rope and my feet on the edge of the cavity, I turned it upon Gordon. He was curled in the foetal position with his arms around a bundle of explosives, and he was weeping softly. I could see the fuse snaking about him ... he had all the appearances of a human bomb.

I had no idea whether his body-bomb was alive or not, but guessed he was able to blow himself to smithereens. And me, if I wasn't careful.

'You'd better get away from here, Nick, I'm going to blow myself up, and this dam and the old bridge and everything else that's ruined my life ... I was so happy, so absolutely happy and then all this happened ...'

'No, Gordon, no. Think of us, everyone, your friends ...'

'And Deirdre? Look what that woman's done to me...'

'She loves you, Gordon,' I had to say. 'She does ... I know she does.'

'How can she? How can she, Nick? If she did, she wouldn't have done what she did,' he sniffed.

'And do you love her?'

'Yes, I do, I do, I do, and I can't live without her.'

'So how can you do this to her? How can you kill yourself in this way, a dreadful

315

way that she'll have to live with for the rest of her life? She's ended her affair, Gordon, I know that. I'm not lying, I wouldn't lie to you! If you love her, you will end this right now. If you do not love her, then by all means go ahead. But she does love you and she loves you dearly ... she's made mistakes; of course, she has, and she knows that. You've made mistakes; this is a mistake but in spite of that, it's you she loves ...'

'You said you're sure she's given him up?' He wiped his eyes with a free hand.

'Yes, I am. I'd swear on the Bible, Gordon, it's all over.'

'Then tell her to come and say so!' The tears began to flow again. 'You tell her that ... tell her to come down here, on that rope, and say so ...'

'She's right above you now, Gordon, waiting,' I said.

'Here? She knows I'm here, like this?'

'She does.'

'Oh my God. How dreadful ... what a dreadful thing to do.' The fact she was so close to him seemed to snap him out of his black mood. 'Nick, help me, for God's sake help me ...'

And suddenly he released the explosives.

'It's not wired up,' he whispered, as he tried to control the sobs which racked his body. 'I daren't do it ... I daren't

... I couldn't.' With a quick movement of his arms, he flung the rolls of quarry explosive out of the cavity. They bounced down the slope of the dam as I closed my eyes ... but they did not explode. Those explosives could withstand such shocks; to be exploded, they had to be detonated.

'Deirdre?' I shouted. 'Come to the rails, will you? Gordon wants you to help him...'

As her pale, tear-stained face appeared at the rails, he looked up at her with his tears blurring the image. 'Do you really love me?' he whispered hoarsely.

'Oh, Gordon, of course I do ... please come home, now.'

He waited and I wondered if he was going to persist in his demand for her to descend to the cavity, but he seized my hand and said, 'Thanks, Nick. Help me up, will you?'

With an easy grace he climbed the steep slope of the dam with me puffing behind as I clutched at the rope which was my lifeline. As we climbed, he gazed at Deirdre whose figure was framed in the dark shape of the old pack-horse bridge and tears flowed freely from both. I hoped the others had had the wisdom to disappear into the darkness and to leave the stage clear for Gordon and Deirdre. Thankfully, they had done so. Gordon climbed over the rails and literally fell into her arms and I heard her say, 'Come on, Gordon, take me home.'

As I regained the security of the walkway, I watched them move slowly away, remaining beneath the old packhorse bridge until they were out of sight, and then Sergeant Blaketon and the others emerged from the shadows.

'He'll need treatment,' were Blaketon's first words.

'He needs Deirdre,' was my response.

Gordon was not convicted, the court recommending treatment for his mental condition and he was soon painting delightfully fresh pictures of the moors and reservoir. Deirdre continued to work but Ken Rigby left once the dam was complete. Warwick Humbert Ravenswood was interred and a plaque marked his final resting place. It was balanced architecturally with a similar one at the other end of the dam which announced it was Ramsdale Bridge Reservoir, along with the dates of construction and the name of the person who performed the opening ceremony, i.e. the Countess of Ramsdale.

Claude's caravan project never materialized, due to concerns among conservationists that his patch of rare *gentiana nivalis* might be harmed, but the reservoir is now a popular tourist attraction with water sports and wild life.

This Large Print Book for the Partially sighted, who cannot read normal print, is published under the auspices of

THE ULVERSCROFT FOUNDATION

THE ULVERSCROFT FOUNDATION

. . . we hope that you have enjoyed this Large Print Book. Please think for a moment about those people who have worse eyesight problems than you . . . and are unable to even read or enjoy Large Print, without great difficulty.

You can help them by sending a donation, large or small to:

The Ulverscroft Foundation, 1, The Green, Bradgate Road, Anstey, Leicestershire, LE7 7FU, England.
or request a copy of our brochure for more details.

The Foundation will use all your help to assist those people who are handicapped by various sight problems and need special attention.

Thank you very much for your help.